sl

KITTY
SLADE

Divine Freaks

phantorama *n*. Very rare condition which gives the ability to see ghosts. Can be cool, but mostly just freaky…

Divine Freaks

fiona dunbar

ORCHARD BOOKS

ORCHARD BOOKS
338 Euston Road, London NW1 3BH
Orchard Books Australia
Level 17/207 Kent Street, Sydney, NSW 2000

First published in the UK in 2011 by Orchard Books

ISBN 978 1 40830 928 5

Text © Fiona Dunbar 2011

A CIP catalogue record for this book is available from the British Library.

3 5 7 9 10 8 6 4 2

Printed in Great Britain by CPI Bookmarque, Croydon

Orchard Books is a division of Hachette Children's Books,
an Hachette UK company.

www.hachette.co.uk

For Helena – you are more of an inspiration
than you know

Rat-Man

People say a lot of stupid things about ghosts.

Let's face it, people do say dumb things about stuff they *think* they know about, but don't. And most people don't actually know the first thing about ghosts. How can I be so sure? Because I know quite a lot about ghosts – I see them all the time.

Number one stupid thing people say: they don't really exist, you know.

OK, just because *they* haven't seen them, doesn't mean they're not there.

Number two: they do exist, but only in old castles and stuff.

Wrong! They're everywhere – on the streets, in supermarkets…in schools. *Your* school, probably.

I haven't always seen ghosts. The first thirteen years of my life were a complete ghost-free zone.

Then things…changed.

Here's how it started.

I was in biology class, minding my own business, when all of a sudden this man appeared, about to murder a rat.

Not a nasty sewer rat or anything, but a lovely snowy white one, really cute. Poor thing was totally freaking out, waving its little pink paws about and gazing up with red beady eyes at this great shining scalpel blade about to slit it open.

The man – tall and hunched, with a mean grey face – just grinned hard. He was going to enjoy this.

Or he would have done, if I'd given him half a chance.

'Nooooo!' I cried, and ran over, sending my stool crashing to the ground. Mr Wesley was blocking my way so I had to shove him aside, which was a bit not-OK, really; he fell against the cabinet full of jars of random body parts in formaldehyde.

Rat-Man grinned his sickly grin, all sallow grey skin and yellow teeth, and then–

I lunged, but he wasn't there any more. I fell in a heap on the floor. He'd disappeared, along with the rat. *Poof!* Just like that. Gone.

'What in the name of…?' began Mr Wesley, as he

adjusted his glasses, his tie, his hair. The cabinet had survived, just.

The whole class was staring at me.

'I wanted to stop him…that man.'

'*What* man?'

Stifled giggles around the class, and I was thinking, what the hell's so funny about a creepy stranger suddenly appearing, wielding a scalpel? But Mr Wesley hadn't seen him…and neither, it seemed, had anyone else. They thought I was just mucking about – which, to be honest, I've been known to do when things have got like, really dull.

'There was a man,' I explained, getting up. 'He was just here! He was…' I gazed around: nothing. I blinked, rubbed my eyes.

Then all of a sudden he appeared again, this time in the corner of the room, by the door. 'There he is…over there!' I yelled.

Everyone turned to look.

He wasn't holding the rat this time. He just stood there, like he was ready to fend off an attacker or something. His vampire face was hard and violent now; the grin was gone. He held up his right hand, and in it glinted something shiny and sharp; the scalpel.

9

I froze, just staring at him...I couldn't believe my eyes.

More giggles from the class. *No, I'm not kidding this time!* I wanted to say...but I was dumbstruck. How was it that only I could see him? There he was, clear as day! Big, ugly – and poised, apparently, for something a whole lot worse than rat-killing. Was I going crazy?

'Kitty Slade, I've had quite enough of you and your idiotic fantasies,' barked Mr Wesley, 'and I will *not* have you disrupt my class! Now go back to your seat.'

'But he's right *there*. He's...oh no...' Rat-Man was coming towards me now. I turned and dived behind Mr Wesley, clutching his jacket. Still Rat-Man came forward, staring wildly at someone or something that I couldn't see, knife at the ready.

I squealed and threw myself on the floor, pulling Mr Wesley down with me. This time his glasses fell right off – and his hair nearly did, too. I shuffled over to his desk and hid under it, as the crazed man lurched wildly around, stabbing the air with his scalpel.

'Everybody! Hide!' I yelled.

They didn't, of course. They only laughed louder. Kitty was on stellar form, ha, ha! They were loving it – especially since this was one of *Mr Wesley's* lessons,

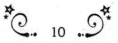

which are typically so boring that you gradually merge with the furniture. You can't even feel sorry for him, 'cause he's a mean old grouch, too.

Normally, I'd have loved an uproar like this – not this time. Still, Mr Wesley wasn't having any of it. I was just mucking about as usual, as far as he was concerned.

I huddled there in my cubby-hole under the desk, my head in a spin. You know that thing your eyes do when you go from brightness into darkness – the way those shapes like negative images and firecracker lights appear in front of you? That was happening too. Then I realised that the actual wood of the desk was changing shape; something luminous was pressing forward from the flat surface…Rat-Man's face.

I didn't scream. I was…transfixed. It was just his face, nothing else. And this time the gleaming, red-rimmed eyes were staring straight at me – like he was trying to tell me something. His mouth was moving, but no sound was coming out.

'What's that?' I asked, but still the mouth moved soundlessly. 'Who are you?' I tried again – though don't ask me why. It was obvious he couldn't make himself heard.

And then the face shrivelled back, flattening out…until it disappeared completely.

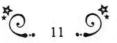 11

Meanwhile, some of my friends seemed to have figured out that I was not mucking about; this was for real. Ella and Deniece came over. 'Kitty?' said Ella. 'It's all right, there's nothing there.'

I peeped out. Rat-Man hadn't reappeared anywhere else in the room. I sighed and got out from under the desk.

Mr Wesley, brushing himself down for a second time, was not in the least bit sympathetic. (See? Mean old grouch.) In fact, he looked as if he was about to explode. 'You two!' he spluttered, jabbing a finger in my friends' direction. 'Back to your seats!'

'But Mr Wesley, she—'

'And you!' – now The Finger was pointed at me – 'To the head teacher's office. Now!'

A strange, hot sensation flooded over me. 'But you don't understand, sir, I—'

'I – said – NOW!'

Fear had me trembling still – now rage was making it worse. 'Why won't you let me explain?'

Mr Wesley's lips were thin and tight. 'Out!'

For a moment, I just stood glaring at him. Couldn't he *see* how shaken up I was? Didn't he have a milligram of sympathy in that podgy little frame of his? No, apparently not.

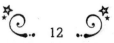

'OK!' I said at last. 'You know what? I AM going out.' I returned to my place at the bench, collected my jacket and backpack and stomped out. 'That's it. I'm out of here!'

Phantorama

I headed home in a daze. Hot with anger one moment, breaking out in shivers the next...then came stabs of self-pity.

I was going crazy – I had to be.

Weaving through the shoppers on Portobello Road, I thought, *Hey everybody, there's a lunatic among you!* But then...any one of them might be crazy, too. Actually, some of them clearly were. You get all sorts in our neighbourhood – the drunks, the punks...that woman in the purple turban with the red lipstick smeared across her face. Would I end up like her? I shuddered at the thought.

Just past the place where the fruit-and-veg stalls end and the antique shops begin, was Eaton Antiques. Home. Well, the flat above it. It was always easy to tell people how to find our place: you just told them to

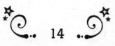

look for the shop with the life-size Beefeater outside. Then first on your left down the alleyway round the corner. Battered old blue door, with the little bronze hand for a knocker.

Heart thumping, I let myself in, and hauled myself up the steep, narrow staircase to our flat. Maro was puttering around in the kitchen with the phone wedged under her chin. Always multi-tasking, is Maro. Which is not necessarily a good thing, let me tell you. The other day when she was chatting to a friend, she put the rubbish in the fridge, and the sausages in the bin. Maro's my gran, but we never *call* her Gran or anything like that. Actually, since she's Greek, the proper term would be *YiaYia*, but we call her by her name, Maro, 'cause…well, she just *is* Maro – there's no one else like her. One in a million, she is. Never mind that she can barely afford to keep us all clothed; she's as chirpy as a sparrow most of the time. Unless she's in a strop, that is. Maro does a proper meltdown when she wants to – which can be hilarious, I've got to say.

As soon as she spotted me, she wrapped up the call. 'Darling, I've got to go, something's come up…call you back later, sweetie, OK? Bye bye! Love yoooo!' (This is how Maro speaks to pretty much everyone.) '*Mwah, mwah,*' she said finally, then put the phone down.

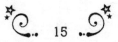

'Kitty…what's up, *pethaki-mou*? How come you're home so early?'

I slumped into the nearest chair. 'I walked out. Maro, something really freaky happened, and I'm…I'm confused…' I felt a lump rise in my throat. 'And I hate Mr Wesley! He wouldn't even *listen*, and…' I couldn't go on. I just dissolved into a blubbing mess.

'All right, sweetie,' said Maro, stroking my hair. 'I'll make you some hot chocolate, and you can tell me all about it.'

My brother Sam appeared, hobbling along on crutches. He'd broken his leg a while back, which was highly ironic, since *I'm* the one that usually gets into scrapes – *he's* the one who's always sitting around reading or watching movies. Not much preparation for collisions with seventy-kilo centre forwards on the school football pitch, I reckon. Sam's in Year Eight, so half the boys in his year have sprouted like beanstalks, while the other half are still little sprogs. Sam was just starting to sprout, and his feet had suddenly got really ugly.

'Hey, what happened?' he said.

I took a deep breath and told them all about the strange man in Mr Wesley's class. 'So you see?' I said at last. 'I must be going crazy.'

'No, you're not,' said Maro firmly.

'But no one else could see him! I must have been like, hallucinating, or something.'

'Trust me, *Kitaki-mou*, you are *not* going crazy.' Maro sounded adamant.

'How can you be so sure–'

'Hey,' Sam interrupted. 'What about the other day, when we were in the game shop–'

'Oh my god, you're right,' I said, suddenly remembering. 'I saw that woman and I asked her for some help, and you couldn't see her at all.'

Maro looked startled. 'What? You never told me about that!'

Her reaction made my face flush hot, and my breath shorten. 'It…didn't seem important at the time.'

'But y'know, there *might've* been a woman – it's possible I just missed her,' said Sam. 'I wasn't looking at first so I thought she must've just been in a hurry and not heard Kitty speaking to her, or…something…'

Maro just stood there, gazing at me.

'Oh god,' I said. 'I *am* going crazy, aren't I?'

'No, no, no,' insisted Maro. She flung her arms around me and gave me a squeeze. 'Oh, my baby!' she cried. 'I was waiting to see if this would happen, and it has. It has!'

'If *what* would happen?'

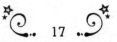 17

Maro wiped away a tear and sniffed. 'They're ghosts, *agapi-mou*; you're seeing ghosts.'

Which of course you know already. But it was the first I'd heard, and…well, I was gobsmacked. '*Ghosts?*' I repeated. 'No…they can't be! I mean, that's impossible…isn't it? Anyway, how come no one else saw that guy in the classroom? Surely if he was a ghost, everyone would see him? I mean, not that there's any such *thing* of course, but–'

'I'm absolutely sure it was a ghost,' said Maro, smiling now.

'And the woman in the game shop?'

'And her too,' said Maro.

'But I *told* you, no one else saw them!'

Then came the bombshell: 'Kitty, I know, because your mamma had the same gift.'

Sam and I both gasped. 'You're kidding me,' I said softly.

There was a deep sadness in Maro's eyes, as there always was when Mum was mentioned – the daughter she'd lost.

Well, at least I'm not crazy, I thought. Though somehow that didn't make me feel a whole lot better about the situation.

'Ghosts. Oh wow…real live ghosts!'

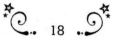

'Er, *dead* ones, Kitty,' said Sam. He shook his head slowly, wide-eyed. 'This is really freaky.'

Meanwhile I was pacing a trench into the kitchen floor. 'It's incredible! In broad daylight…in *biology class*… Ha! I thought these things just happened at night, in spooky old houses–'

'Not that you really thought they ever happened at all,' Sam remarked.

'Not that I really thought they happened at all,' I said, at the same time. I stopped in my tracks. 'But how? Why? What are we going to do about it?'

Maro explained the whole thing to me. 'There are those who can communicate with the spirits without seeing them – the mediums – and those are rare enough. The genuine ones, at least. And then there are people like you and your mamma – even rarer. We have a word for it in Greek: *phantorama*. The ghosts just appear to you, in all sorts of situations – often without you asking them to. And just the same as you, your mother first began to experience it when she was thirteen. That's how it happens, you know; when you're getting the pubation–'

'You mean *puberty*, Maro,' I said, cringing. Maro's been living in England for over forty years, but deep down she's as Greek as a lamb souvlaki and she comes

out with some real howlers sometimes.

'Never mind that!' said Sam. 'What about me? Am I going to get the same thing?'

Being just a year younger than me, you could see why he would be a bit panicked.

'For some reason, boys don't seem to develop it,' said Maro.

'Oh,' said Sam. He frowned. 'Hmm...not sure whether to be relieved or jealous, to be honest. Hey, what about–'

'Flossie?' said Maro. Flossie's our sister, who's ten. 'No, the odds are against Flossie getting it. As I say, it's very rare. But not impossible.'

'Hang on: do *you* have it?' said Sam.

'Me?' Maro laughed. 'Oh no. I think you'd have known that by now! I should have explained – it comes from your *grandfather's* side of the family.'

I was still taking it all in. And suddenly, a penny dropped. 'Hang on. You knew about this all along, and you never said anything!'

Maro took my empty mug and busied herself with washing it out. 'I thought best not to, sweetie. Imagine how distracting it would be, always wondering when the ghosts were going to start popping up – when it was probably never going to happen.'

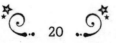

Well, I could see she had a point. I calmed down a bit. 'Phantorama…ha! Sounds like a 3D movie, or something. And is it *just* seeing, or do we communicate ever? The Rat-Man seemed like he was trying to talk to me.'

'Things will…develop from here,' said Maro. 'Though it's hard to know how long it will take. It varies, I'm told. You may hear some of them speak, but they won't be able to interact with you. Others might actually talk to you – eventually. If you're lucky. I mean…well, depending on how you look at it. Oh, and one more thing – you may come into physical contact with them from time to time, but try not to. Apparently it's not a pleasant sensation.' Then she took me by the shoulders and looked me squarely in the eye. 'And never, *ever* link hands with a ghost. Do you understand? *Never.*'

'Why?'

'Because if you do, you may be risking your life.'

'Oh.'

Wow.

This was major. I didn't know whether to feel special and happy and privileged or…none of those things. Part of me just wanted to wind the film back to when things were normal. Because the fact was, life was never going to be normal for me again.

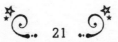

And questions were tripping over each other in my head. One thing in particular was really starting to trouble me. 'What about my mum?' I asked. 'What if I see...' I couldn't finish the sentence. The thought of coming face-to-face with the ghost of my own mother was...well, thrilling, maybe, but troubling as well. Would I even recognise her? After all, I didn't really remember her – neither did Sam. The accident happened when we were so little. Flossie was just a baby. By now we really didn't have much more than a vague *sense* of her; a sort of echo of a spirit.

'You won't ever see your mamma's ghost,' Maro said gently. 'You see, people with phantorama never appear in spirit form themselves. No one knows why. But in your grandfather's family they believe that it's because their spirits are always quickly reabsorbed into the physical world. Nature makes this happen, because only in the living world can they do their valuable work of connecting between the living and the dead.'

'So our mum is...someone else now,' I said.

'According to the Slade family tradition she would be, yes,' said Maro. 'And I for one am happy to believe that. My darling Effie lives on, somewhere!' Her eyes went all glassy again. 'Oh, enough of this!' she said briskly. 'I need to speak to your school about the

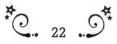

whole biology class business.'

She reached for the phone, but it rang before she got the chance to pick it up. She jumped. 'Hello? Ah yes, I was just going to call you…' She put her hand over the mouthpiece and whispered, 'It's the head teacher,' before moving into the next room.

I caught Sam's eye and made a face.

'It'll be all right,' he said.

'No it won't. There's all the other stuff.'

'You mean, like the time you electrocuted the DT teacher when you were making those circuits?'

'I only meant to give him a little *bzzt*!' I said. 'Just to see his reaction. How was I to know it would throw him across the room?'

'…And the times you've gone AWOL in lunch break…'

'Well, all right, I know there's no excuse for that one. But that's exactly my point – they didn't buy it then, and they're not buying it now…'

I didn't finish, as Maro's voice was getting really loud. 'I can assure you, sir, that it most certainly *was* a ghost!' she yelled. '…Because I know! OK, you know what? I don't think there's any point in me coming in for a meeting…no, forget it. If you're telling me that you won't even consider such an explanation…oh, really? Is

that so? Well, fine, sir. That's just fine with us. She doesn't ever want to come back again anyway!'

Maro came back into the kitchen, looking wound up.

'OK, I think I know roughly what that was all about,' I said.

'Ha! That man! He was only calling me in to tell me you're suspended for the rest of the term. He'd already made up his mind.'

'I take it he doesn't believe in ghosts,' said Sam.

'Doesn't believe, won't listen, says Kitty's just a troublemaker…well, I don't care. I don't care!' Maro waved her arms around melodramatically, then threw them around me. 'Never you mind, baby, mmmm-wah!' She gave me a big kiss on the head. 'It's going to be OK.'

Right.

How the hell was I going to get used to this?

Eaton Alive

Wow, this is weird. Me! Doing a blog! SO not like me. The only people I know who blog are either:

a) Saddos like Fenella Armstrong, who blathers on about how she wishes she had a boyfriend/can't afford the clothes she wants/hates her life, or

b) Over-achievers like Kate McKenzie, who boasts about scoring the winning goal in netball etc etc.

The difference is, I'm not posting this one online: it's private. I WANT to talk to my friends about this…but I can't. Not even Ella. She keeps phoning and texting, but all I do is stare at the screen trying to figure out what to say, then find I can't go through with it. I mean, what use would it be, anyway? It's not like she can give me

any advice or comfort – she has NO IDEA what this is like! The truth is, only someone else with phantorama could possibly understand, and I don't know anyone who has it.

So here goes: today I saw my first ghost. Well, not strictly speaking the first – but he might just as well be. Maybe I've seen others wafting among the crowds in the street...who knows? I don't THINK I saw any on my way back from school but then I was so freaked out I probably wouldn't have noticed someone coming down the street stark naked, riding an ostrich.

Anyway: the ghost. Rat-Man, I'm calling him. Please, please don't let the others be as horrible as him. Maro tells me they won't be...she says ghosts come in all varieties, same as live people. Some are nice, some aren't. 'The two things they all have in common,' she said, 'is that they're dead, and they all have unfinished business.' They've failed to make it over to the spirit world, and they're lingering on earth because they're desperate to get something done – something they didn't have the chance to do while they were still alive.

So the question is: *what is Rat-Man's unfinished business?* What was he trying to say to me? Do I really want to know?

OMG, I've just realised it's time for me to go and pick up Flossie from ballet – I have to face the outside world again. Plus ghosts, from now on. I can't face it. What if...argh.

OK, deep breath.

You're stuck with this thing now: you might as well get used to it.

GO, Kitty.

'A ghosht?' spluttered Flossie, spitting bits of apple. She jumped off the low wall she'd been walking along and started going backwards in front of me instead. 'What, a *real* one?' Her coat hung halfway down her back over her pink ballet outfit, and she gazed at me with her big brown eyes.

I gave her a withering look. 'There's such a thing as a *fake* ghost?'

'Of course there is,' said Flossie, pulling the scrunchie out of her hair. 'You know, like at Halloween?'

'We're not talking person-with-a-sheet-over-their-head, Floss! You tell me when anyone has managed to disappear into thin air for a party trick!'

Flossie's dark-honey hair flopped in front of her face. She tucked it behind her ear. 'Wow. I mean, really! *Wow.*'

Just then, this woman in flowing beige robes came across the pavement and stepped right out into the road, in front of an oncoming car. I lunged forward, yelling, 'Watch out!'

But she didn't react, and neither did the driver, and the car just ploughed right into her…then she melted into thin air.

I stood there, mouth open.

'You all right, love?' said a guy who was packing up his market stall nearby.

'Um, yeah…' I said, but I trailed off. I was only just getting to grips with what had happened.

He leaned on a crate of oranges, head cocked to one side. 'You sure? You look like you've seen a ghost!'

'No, I just thought someone was going to get run over, but they weren't. I'm fine, really…thanks,' I muttered, feeling completely bewildered.

Flossie took my hand and led me away. 'You *did* see a ghost, didn't you?' she said when we were a few metres down the road,

'Yes…'

'And what's it *like*, seeing ghosts?'

'Right now, I'd say it's like being surrounded by sharks in one of those cages they send cameramen down in. I know they're probably not going to touch

me…I suppose I know somehow that they're not going to *hurt* me. But all the same, it's freaky!'

We went round the corner and down the slope of Portobello Road. The sun was low in the sky. Outside the Moroccan café, the usual gang of men were sitting, smoking. The fabric-seller was shutting up shop, lugging in the hulking great rolls of fabric. Same as usual. The air reeked of fumes from all the commuters in their cars who were starting to head home to the suburbs. Just as they always did, day in, day out. It all seemed…normal. And here I was, looking around at them all and thinking, 'Guys! You have ghosts wandering around among you all the time, and you have *no idea!*'

'It's going to be very distracting if it carries on this way,' I told Flossie.

'Maybe there's some sort of medicine or pills you can get for it,' she suggested. 'Why don't you go to the doctor?'

'Yeah, *right*,' I said. '"Hey, doc, I keep seeing ghosts" – "Never mind, here's a prescription for Ghost-Away tablets"… OK, now *that* one's got to be a ghost.' I watched as a woman in a crinoline and powdered wig sailed past the Rastafarian clothing store, holding up one of those specs-on-sticks things and peering at the red,

gold and green hats on display. Sure enough, she vanished in an instant.

I stood and stared, vaguely aware of Flossie saying something about wanting to know what I saw, but I was just…well, dumbfounded, thinking, *how am I going to get used to this?*

Then I noticed her hand waving in front of my face. 'Earth to Kitty…!'

'Sorry…sorry. It's just been the weirdest day,' I explained as we walked on. 'Got a lot on my mind, what with this whole ghost thing, getting expelled from school…'

'What? You got *expelled*?'

'Um…sort of. Basically we fell out, and I'm not going back.' Remembering this kind of cheered me up. 'Yay! I'm never going back! No more schoo-oo-ool!'

'But won't you have to go to another one?' asked Flossie.

'Nope! Maro's gonna home-school me. She's been doing that with Sam ever since his accident anyway, so as far as she's concerned, what's the diff. Which is completely brilliant, 'cause she mainly does the fun stuff.'

'Hey, not fair!' cried Flossie. 'What about me? Do I still have to go to school?'

'Well, yes–' I began, but just then this whacking

great maroon Jaguar appeared alongside us, purring expensively.

'I say!' called the driver. 'If it isn't the Misses Slade!'

It was Roderick Eaton, owner of Eaton Antiques, the shop we lived above. All the Portobello stallholders knew him – he seemed to think he was the bee's knees, though none of us could stand him. He had huge, droopy-lidded eyes and a wide mouth, like a gigantic toad. Red, bloated face and great bulging belly straining at the buttons on his candy-striped shirt. Bushy eyebrows poking out from underneath a stupid bit of longish fringe that drooped on his forehead like a wilted weed. Definitely in denial about going bald.

Our nickname for him was Eaton Alive.

'Urgh, what the hell does he want?' I said, linking arms with Flossie and moving on swiftly. 'Come on, let's pretend we didn't hear.'

'Looks like a new car,' said Flossie. 'Maybe he wants to show it off.'

'Oh…yeah, probably,' I said, having noted the gleaming chrome trim and the personalised number plate: EAT ON. 'Don't know where the money comes from – have you ever noticed anyone actually *buying* antiques in that shop? The same stuff just sits there.'

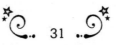

'They move things around a bit sometimes,' said Flossie.

Unfortunately Eaton Alive wasn't going to be put off so easily. As we got to the next junction, he swerved and pulled over, blocking our way.

We were cornered.

'I say! Hello!' he bellowed, lunging his fat head out through the car window and treating us to that big, gap-toothed grin of his. 'Been to ballet, eh? Sweet... sweet! *Nutcracker* and all that...love it! Well, well, how are we, then?'

I forced myself not to be rude. Maro had said it wouldn't do to fall out with him. So I just about managed an 'OK'.

'Matter of fact, glad I caught you,' said Eaton. 'Is your grandmamma around, by any chance? Spot of business to discuss, dontcha know.'

What? I thought. This was a new one. I decided to spare Maro. 'No, she's out shopping,' I lied. 'I've no idea what time she's coming back.'

'Hmm...' Roderick gazed suspiciously at me with that toad-like stare of his, which was very unnerving. 'Never mind!' he said at last. 'We'll soon catch up. I'll give her a call. Toodle-oo!' He drove off.

'He's going round there right now, I bet you

anything,' I said. I pulled out my phone and called Maro. 'Eaton Alive alert! He's coming to see you at home, says he's got a "spot of business" to discuss.'

'He's coming *here*?' asked Maro. 'Why?'

'I dunno,' I said, adding jokily, 'maybe he's thinking of proposing to you.'

'Ugh, stop it!' cried Maro, laughing. 'Well, thanks for the warning. Maybe I'll just not answer the door.'

But Roderick Eaton obviously managed to weasel his way in somehow, because when we got home there he was, at the kitchen table with a mug of tea, all sprawled out and taking up nearly all the space in the tiny room like he owned the place.

'Ha ha!' he gloated, as we walked in. 'Seems your grandmamma had a change of plan!'

Maro gave me a long-suffering glance from the kitchen counter, where she was trying to get supper ready.

Sam hobbled in from his bedroom on his crutches, and picked up a ruler from the table. 'Uh…hi,' he mumbled, not really looking at Eaton.

'Hello, it's the young invalid!' said Eaton. 'Well, well, now, I see the cast is off. Back at school yet, then?'

'Not till after Easter,' said Sam.

'Splendid, splendid. And you'll be off playing footie again in no time, I'll bet – won't he, Grandma?'

A curt 'yes' was all he got out of Maro; she'd given up asking him not to call her 'Grandma' some time ago.

'Yes…big, open spaces, that's what a young lad like you needs,' Eaton went on. 'Ever thought of moving out to the suburbs, Grandma?'

I dumped my bag and went over to help Maro prepare the veg. I gave her a look. What a nosey old fart. Not to mention rude! If this was Eaton's idea of how you did friendly chit-chat, I reckoned he needed to go on a course or something.

'Not in a million years,' said Maro. 'I've always lived in this part of town. I love it here. The kids do, too.'

'Yeah,' we said.

Yeah, bog off with your stupid suburbia talk, I thought. I loved the way our part of London was villagey and city-ish at the same time. So quiet early on a Sunday morning down our little cobbled mews with its pretty pastel-coloured cottages – you could imagine how it was in the olden days, with horses and carts and everything.

Then there was the bustle of Saturday afternoons, with all the stalls selling everything from vintage dolls to military paraphernalia. OK, so the tourists got on my nerves sometimes, always stopping suddenly to take

pictures and stuff. But mostly I loved it. And on a rainy day, the best thing was the indoor stalls; you could dive into this cavernous warren of them, a real Aladdin's Cave of antique lace, stuffed birds and mechanical tin toys. It smelled of boot polish and silver dip and musty cupboards, and you could spend ages just wandering about and imagining the past lives connected to these things. I suddenly wondered what it would it be like to go around there now, with my phantorama...

'And your home country?' Eaton was still harping on. 'Ever thought of moving back to Greece? Lovely place!'

'No,' said Maro sharply. 'We like it here. Why are you asking–'

Eaton wasn't listening. '...Blue skies, sparkling sea, whitewashed hilltop villages...ah! Wouldn't mind living there myself!'

'Well, why don't you move there, then?' replied Maro.

'Ha ha, well I might, well I might...one day, when I retire. But business is booming, Mrs S. In fact–' Eaton's phone rang. Impatiently, he pulled it from his jacket pocket and switched it off. 'Ahem, fact of the matter is, Mrs S,' he said, pocketing the phone again, 'I have a business matter to discuss.'

Maro didn't look up, just went right on chopping the beans. 'I'm not interested in doing business with you, Mr Eaton, so if that's what you came here to discuss, then I–'

Eaton got up from his chair, scraping it across the floor. Maro looked up, alarmed.

'I'll cut to the chase, Mrs S,' he said. 'I'm expanding my business, upwards' – he gestured with flattened hands – 'so I'm giving you notice that I've bought this flat from your landlady, Mrs Kyriakou, and you're going to have to move out.'

Maro's knife slammed hard at the beans on the chopping board, sending the tips flying off. She turned to him with fire in her eyes. '*What* did you say?'

'Such is the way of business, Mrs S – but London is teeming with places to rent, you'll soon find something else!'

'Something else? But I don't *want* something else, Mr Eaton. We're fine here. Besides, I can't afford a…that is, I…'

'Ah, yes…I looked into your, uh, little "rental arrangement"' – Eaton drew quotation marks in the air – 'with your friend Mrs Kyriakou. Somewhat… unofficial, shall we say?'

Maro's face turned to stone.

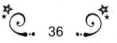

I felt my own face go all prickly, as I pictured her monthly ritual of reaching under her mattress for the rent she always paid Mrs Kyriakou in tens and twenties. It had been done the same way for as long as I could remember – and I never used to think anything of it. It didn't exactly bother me, even if I did realise it probably wasn't the way things were usually done. And I knew that Maro always turned a blind eye to things like damp patches, dripping taps and drawers that didn't shut, because she was being charged far less rent than she should have been.

Sam, Floss and I looked at each other nervously. This did not look good.

'This is outrageous!' snapped Maro, reaching for the phone and hitting the speed-dial.

'Oh, I'm afraid that won't do any good, Mrs S,' said Eaton. His smarmy look hardened into something darker; his toad-like eyes looked fierce and penetrating, and the oily smile was gone. 'I understand Mrs Kyriakou is unwell at present – she's in hospital.' Eaton nudged a loose electric powerpoint over the counter. It came away easily in his hand. 'Hmm…wiring a bit ropey, isn't it?'

Then he opened the boiler cupboard, and the door promptly fell half off its hinges. 'And when was the last

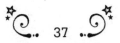

time the boiler was inspected by an engineer?'

'Six months ago!' cried Maro, still with the phone wedged under her chin as she searched in a drawer. 'Her son takes care of it…here,' she said, pulling out a hand-written certificate of inspection and passing it to Eaton.

He gave it the barest glance. 'Tut-tut-tut…not worth the paper it's printed…er, *written* on. The same goes for your "contract" with Mrs Kyriakou. The truth is, you have no legal standing in this matter, Mrs S – none whatsoever. You have one month to get out–'

'A month! How dare you–'

We all started to protest too.

Maro abandoned the phone and moved closer to Eaton, not really noticing that she was still holding the kitchen knife. 'You can threaten all you like, Mr Eaton. We're – not – budging!'

Eaton backed away, warily eyeing the blade as it sliced through the air. 'All right, steady on, steady on. You know, if you were to make me a *very* attractive buy-out offer, I might reconsider–'

'I don't have the money!' shrieked Maro. 'Now, if you don't mind, I am making *to vrathi*. It's dinnertime, so good evening to you, *piyainete*!'

And out he went. Maro slammed the door after him.

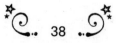

The Tyburn Ghosts

OK, so my life has suddenly got itself into such a huge mess, I don't dare think about what's going to happen next. First the phantorama, now all this business with Eaton Alive. God, I hate him so much! Maro says not to worry about getting kicked out, she'll work something out. I only hope she can...

Anyway: this is meant to be my GHOST blog, so that's what I'm going to concentrate on. (Thought: is it a coincidence that all these things are happening at once? Is there anything I can DO about it?!)

OK, Rat-Man:

1. Who IS he??! I mean, WAS.
2. Why was he haunting the science lab?

3. One minute he was about to dissect a rat, and the next he was apparently fighting off an attacker with his scalpel. WHY??

4. And who was he fighting off?

5. Then his face followed me around, and tried to tell me something. What?

FIND OUT ANSWERS TO THESE QUESTIONS.

Problem: have been excluded from school. This could be a bit of a drawback.

God, I really want to call Ella, but it's too late now. Anyway I CAN'T tell her about Rat-Man! I know. I'll say it was a migraine, one of those unbelievable headaches that start out with flashing lights, distorted vision and stuff. I've never had one, but I bet they're almost as scary as seeing a ghost.

Maybe I'll tell Ella the truth one day – just not yet. She'd only be dying to tell Deniece, probably wouldn't be able to help herself, and then, and then…before you knew it, the whole world would know.

It's just you and me, blog. Password protected.

It took me ages to get to sleep that night, even though I was knackered. Still couldn't stop worrying about getting kicked out of our home, and where we might

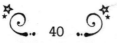

move to. Maro said not to worry, she'd sort it out – but it was hard not to.

I gazed enviously at Flossie in her bed across the room, slumbering blissfully like a baby with her teddy. If only a nice cuddly toy were all it took for me to feel so comforted…

I slept late next morning – not even the alarm or Flossie getting ready for school disturbed me.

I looked at the clock: 10.30! Brilliant. Back at school they'd all have sat through double maths and geography by now, ha ha. Bliss. For a moment I felt a pang of guilt – but it soon passed. I got up and shuffled into the kitchen to make some tea, took a fistful of biscuits and wandered into Sam's room.

'Hey, lazybones,' he said. He was sitting by the large window, notepad on his lap.

'Yeah, well, I'm kind of *stressed*, you know? It's tiring.'

'I know. Sorry.'

'S'OK.'

Sam chewed his lip and gazed at me. 'I don't know how I'd feel if it was me. In a way it's kind of cool. But then…that must've been really freaky, what happened in biology class. I wonder what that Rat-Man ghost was doing there?'

I shrugged. 'I don't know.' Rat-Man had been doing

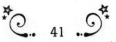

my head in all night. By now I really didn't feel like talking about it. I changed the subject. 'What're you doing?'

Sam held up the notepad. 'Maths. This is a school day for me, remember. Been up three hours already. Maro's only giving you the one day off. Tomorrow you'll be up with the rest of us.'

'I know, I know. Where is Maro, anyway?'

'It's breaktime. She's gone to see Mrs Kyriakou about this whole Eaton business.' He glanced at the clock. 'And I've got to get this lot finished before she gets back, so bog off, Kit.' He turned and hunched over his notepad.

Ha! So much for sympathy; back to the same old Mr No-Fun Swot in no time minus five. He *is* a bit of a swot, my brother – which can make him a bit superior sometimes, never mind that he's younger than me. He thinks he's so grown up, but he's still got a pile of teddies and Spot the Dogs in the corner of his room.

I didn't feel like leaving just yet. I wanted company, even if it meant hanging out with Mr Swotty Swot-Face. I sat down on the beanbag – kind of heavily, which made it do that satisfying *whuf-fuffle* thing that beanbags do.

Sam shot me an irritated look.

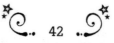

'So-rree!' I said. He went back to his maths problems.

I gazed around the room, munching on my Rich Tea biscuit. So if I was having a day off, what should I do with it? Sit around and watch movies all day? Actually, that was a pretty good idea...

Sam had collected quite a stack of DVDs while he'd been housebound with the broken leg. I gazed along his dusty, overstuffed shelves, checking them out. Boring. I must've groaned out loud (didn't mean to) 'cause then he looked up again and *sighed* at me.

'OK, I'm going,' I said. 'Just trying to find a DVD to watch, that's all. Why are you so obsessed with all these old black and white movies, anyway?'

''Cause they're brilliant stories, that's why,' said Sam. 'Detective stories. You should give them a chance, you know.'

I pulled out one called *The Maltese Falcon*. The cover showed this ancient actor called Humphrey Bogart in a trilby hat, holding a gun. 'I'll tell you the real reason you like them,' I said. 'It's ever since you discovered you have nearly the same name as this detective' – I waggled the DVD at him – 'Sam Spade'.

Sam rolled his eyes. 'Oh yeah, right, that's the *only* reason.'

I ignored his sarcasm and pulled out another DVD,

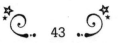

called *Rear Window*. 'So who are you, Sam?' I asked. 'Sam Spade or this guy…what's his name?'

'Jeff Jeffries. Kitty–'

'Jeff Jeffries, that's it!' I'd actually seen this one: it was one of the first DVDs Maro had bought after Sam's accident. It's not bad, actually – at least it's in colour, and has a story you can follow without having a degree in complicated-plot-solving. Jeff Jeffries is a photographer who's stuck in his flat with a broken leg. He spends all day looking through his telephoto lens at his neighbours in the block of flats opposite him, 'cause there's like, nothing else to do. Then – *dun dun dunn!* – he witnesses a murder.

'So, Sam,' I said, peering out of his window into the scuzzy old yard below. 'Seen any murders yet?'

'Oh, yeah, I have actually. Didn't I mention it? Horrible, it was – blood everywhere.'

'Ha ha.'

Just then Maro came in. 'Kitty, are you bugging your brother when he's trying to do his maths?'

'No, I–'

'Yes, she is,' said Sam.

'No, we were just chatting,' I told her.

'OK, Kitty, leave him alone, he's got work to do – and now I'm going to set some for you as well.'

'Huh? But you said you were giving me the day off!'

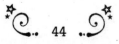

'Not if you're going to be a nuisance.'

I thought for a moment. 'OK, how about I run some errands for you.'

'I've just *been* shopping,' said Maro. 'Among other things.'

I felt slightly ill again as I thought about Roderick Eaton. 'What's going to happen about the flat? Did you see Mrs Kyriakou?'

'Yes,' said Maro brightly. 'Don't worry, *Kitaki-mou.* We'll sort it out.'

I knew that sudden, upbeat smile of hers. It was the one she put on when she was *pretending* everything was fine…

'Ah, I tell you what you can do for me,' she said, moving on quickly. 'Why don't you go to the Middle Eastern store on the Edgware Road. I've run out of cardamom coffee. That'll get you some exercise.'

I shrugged. 'OK.'

'Oh, and Kitty?' said Sam.

'Yes?'

'Get me a kilo of ectoplasm while you're about it, will you?'

I frowned at him. 'A kilo of *what*?'

'Ectoplasm – you know – the stuff ghosts are made of.'

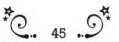

I picked up Spot the Dog and threw it at him. 'Ha ruddy ha.'

It felt good to get out, actually. It was a bright, sunny day, and I suppose I quite liked that I'd been given something to do. And I had on my favourite jacket that was a hand-me-down from Maro – which made it extra cool, 'cause all my friends wanted one like it but you couldn't get one anywhere. It's red leather, which clashed brilliantly with my mismatched striped dayglo over-the-knee socks. I like stuff that clashes; it's my look. I'm known for it at school – or *was*. My classmates always gave me funny looks at first, then started copying me. The teachers hated us going about like that, but I never could get a straight answer out of them about *why* your clothes had to match.

I hit the Bayswater Road, which is this massive wide street running along the top of Hyde Park. It was bursting with daffodils and magnolia blossom. Yeah, this was good. No more school – yay! *Free.*

Then the whole ghost scene from yesterday started playing out in my head all over again, and I felt confused and *so* alone. I wished my mum was around. What had it been like for her? Maro had told me some stories about her experiences the night before, but it wasn't

enough. I wanted *advice*! What were the do's and don'ts of hanging out with spooks?

And there were all those unanswered questions about Rat-Man. It seemed he'd sensed my developing phantorama real time, as it emerged like a chick hatching from an egg. Perhaps he'd been haunting the biology lab all along, then *crack!* My shell had opened, the psychic connection was made, and he thought: *Aha! Now I can tell my story!*

Only, er, I couldn't hear him.

My phantorama, as Maro had pointed out, was still developing. I might have experienced the visual breakthough, but the sound hadn't been switched on yet. Still, one thing I felt sure of: whatever Rat-Man was trying to tell me, it was something important. And however scary he was to me, he'd looked pretty freaked out about something, the second time he'd appeared – like he was about to be attacked himself. Had something terrible happened to him, right there in the school lab?

I needed to find out more. Apart from anything else, it would be *so* brilliant to prove to Mr Wesley that I'd been telling the truth! But how?

I'd just have to find out more on my own, I told myself. One way or another, I would do it. Yes! The thought of investigating gave me a thrill – maybe this

phantorama stuff wasn't so bad after all. It was exciting! What was the matter with me? Why did I have to worry about things all the time? Loads of people would be jealous! *Yes*, I thought – I'm unique, and lucky.

Just then a terrifying figure loomed towards me.

He may have been dressed in fancy clothes from long ago – powdered wig, lace ruffles, silk jacket, those short breeches and white stockings – but other than that he was *horrible*. His head lolled way over to one side, and his eyes bulged so far out they looked ready to pop. His mouth gaped open, overstuffed with a fat lump of meat or something, which I soon realised was actually his tongue.

'Aaargh!' I cried, and leaped out of the way, right into the path of a posh-looking woman walking her dog.

'What in heaven's name…?' said the woman. Her dog began yapping furiously.

The awful man disappeared.

I leaned on the park railings and tried to compose myself. OK, it's a ghost…it's only a ghost, and it's gone now, I told myself. I somehow managed a garbled apology to the woman.

'I'm sorry,' I said. 'There was a…I mean, I…I just remembered something I…I forgot.'

'Huh! Well, you might just exercise a little more

composure, young lady!' The woman marched off indignantly, tugging at the dog's lead.

I was trembling uncontrollably. I took a few deep breaths and tried to rid myself of the horrible lingering image of the man. Finally I calmed down enough to carry on walking.

I reached Marble Arch, the huge monument shining in the sun like some sort of demented wedding cake at the corner of the park. I saw a dark mass of figures milling about: just another bunch of tourists, I supposed. Plenty of them round there, what with Little Cairo (the Edgware Road), the shops and the shops and the shops of Oxford Street, and the great slabs of hotels on Park Lane.

Yeah: tourists.

No: hang on…

This wasn't right. Instead of huddling together around a guide like tourists usually did, this lot were kind of roaming about in different directions. And then I heard sounds coming from them, not happy chatter, but low groans and croaking sounds. Finally the horror struck me, and I realised they were all like the man I'd just seen – decked out in ancient finery, but with crooked necks and bulging eyes and tongues.

I shut my eyes, held my head and cried, 'No, no, no!'

I heard screeching brakes, then a familiar voice.

'Kitty! Get in!'

I opened my eyes, and there, parked at an angle with one wheel up on the kerb, was Maro's beat-up red Ford Fiesta, with Maro beckoning furiously out of the window. I stumbled towards her, threw myself onto the back seat and slammed the door.

'Oh, Kitty, I'm so sorry!' wailed Maro, as she jolted forward, trying to get the old car back into the stream of traffic. 'I should never have sent you down here, I'm really sorry!'

'What? Why? How did you know…'

'Did you see horrible ghosts?' asked Maro.

'Yes! *Horrible*, with bulging eyes, and–'

'Oh, I'm so stupid!' cried Maro. 'It wasn't until I settled down to a history lesson with Sam that I thought of it.'

'Thought of *what*?'

'We're doing the history of London, *Kitaki-mou*, and– Hey! *Vlakas!*' She honked at a driver who'd just cut across in front of her. 'Sorry, Kitty…anyway, when I picked up the book, I suddenly remembered the chapter about prisons, and I realised I'd sent you to almost the same exact spot where…where they used to hang people.'

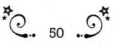

'Eurgh! So that's what I saw? The ghosts of hanged people?'

'I'm afraid so. The gibbet was right about there,' said Maro, pointing towards the Edgware Road. 'The Tyburn, they called it – after the river that ran this way from the Thames. It runs underground now. They brought prisoners all the way up here from Newgate: it would be a big procession, quite a spectacle.'

Someone honked at Maro as she awkwardly tried to change lanes. She honked back.

'Yes, well, *I've* had quite a spectacle,' I said, after she'd finally managed the junction. 'And I never want to see anything like *that* again.'

Maro sighed. 'I'm *so* sorry, baby. It's the people with unfinished business, like I told you. And I suddenly thought, my god, if anyone's likely to have unfinished business, it's going to be someone whose life was cut off in a violent way like that. And sure thing, my worst fears were right.'

'Well, that figures, I guess,' I said, feeling a little calmer now. 'But…didn't you say something last night about my mum somehow screening out ghosts she didn't want to see? How do I do that?'

'Yes, she did do that,' said Maro. 'Only she wasn't able to screen them out completely – just sort of push

them aside, if you know what I mean. And you have to *see* the ghost in the first place, in order to tune it out. Effie said it was like hearing someone else's conversation on a train or a bus. It's possible to escape to a different frequency, like with a radio. But only if you have a book, or a conversation of your own – something to absorb all your concentration. You're still aware of that other conversation somewhere in your head, but it doesn't bother you.'

'Yes, well, there's a big difference between a couple of people chatting on a bus and a bunch of monstrous groaning corpses!' I said.

'I know, but most places you won't have that anyway.'

'Omigod, I just realised something!' I said suddenly.

'What?' said Maro, swerving slightly as she turned to look at me. Usually she was an OK driver, but today she was all over the place.

'The groaning,' I said. 'I *heard* them, Maro!'

'You heard them…and you didn't hear the one at school?'

'No, that's right. I guess the sound got switched on.'

'Well, yes,' said Maro. 'But it's a *process* – not all spirits communicate at the same level, especially at first. It's not as if suddenly it's all a hundred per cent there.

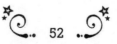

Some will make sound. Some won't. Some will want to communicate with you; others won't – or, like your man yesterday, try and fail. I remember that used to drive Effie crazy! But you learn to screen out the noise as well. Trust me, *pethaki-mou*, it will get a lot more manageable.'

'OK, well…I hope it works for me.'

'It *will* work for you,' said Maro firmly. 'That's a promise. Just keep it in perspective, that's all. It can be a great gift, but make sure *you* control *it*, not the other way round.'

I thought for a moment. 'Maro, you know the ones that try to talk to you, but can't?'

'Yes?'

'Do they sometimes…start out unable to, and then…and then their voices come through later?'

'Probably,' said Maro vaguely. 'Yes, they must do sometimes… Oh no – look at the time! I have to take Sam to the hospital for his physio. Why don't you come with us?'

I looked at her. 'You're kidding, right? Me, go to a *hospital*? Where people have been known to like, die?'

'Oops…good point. Well, they'd mostly have died of natural causes–'

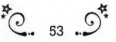

'*No*, Maro.'

'OK, OK…'

We drove on in silence. Meanwhile, my mind was buzzing…

A Warning

Maro and Sam left for the hospital.

I stared at a book Maro had suggested I read, but I kept reading the same sentence over and over, and the words weren't sinking in. All I could think of were those Tyburn ghosts.

I wandered into the living room, turned on the TV and flicked through the channels till I got to XFM. I liked the song that was playing. Actually, I didn't like it – it was annoying. But I liked the dancing.

Sound off.

Sound on.

Sound off. Sound gradually increasing from nothing to full-on blare.

If I saw Rat-Man again, then maybe I'd find out what he was on about. His sound might be switched on by now. OK, but there was no point even thinking about

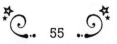

that, because I wouldn't ever be back in that biology lab. I had left. Moved on.

I watched some more XFM, then three episodes of the same dumb sitcom, back-to-back. This was good. Took my mind completely away from gruesome ghosts. Then I went on the computer. Nobody available for chat, of course: school-time. Rats.

Little white lab rats. Rat-Man. Ah, the hell with Rat-Man! I wished I could stop obsessing over what he'd been trying to tell me. Who *was* he?

Out of desperation, I googled 'who is the ghost of gateshill school?'

It brought up only normal links about my school, with no mention of ghosts – followed by a few about ghosts, but not Gateshill. Kind of a dumb thing to search anyway. Maybe there was something else I could try…

OK, number one: what if he'd been a teacher at the school – a biology teacher? Who else would appear in the lab, wearing a white coat and holding a scalpel and a lab rat?

Number two: he'd died leaving unfinished business. Had something happened to him right there in the lab? Maybe he'd died a violent death of some sort, like the Tyburn ghosts. And a violent death would have been reported in the newspaper…

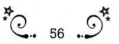

I typed in 'gateshill teacher death'. Again, loads of entries with 'teacher' and 'Gateshill School' but not 'death'. But then, scrolling down, I came across something from the local paper:

SCHOOL'S SHOCK OVER UNTIMELY DEATH OF TEACHER

GATESHILL SCHOOL SCIENCE TEACHER

KILLED IN HIT-AND-RUN ACCIDENT

My mouth dropped open – it all fitted.

The science teacher was called Mr Divine: he'd been knocked down by a hit-and-run driver five years ago. He was rushed to hospital but was dead on arrival. And there, staring out of the computer screen at me, was the face of Rat-Man. The photo had been blown up and cropped from a group picture, so it was all grainy. And unlike his ghostly appearance, he had a relaxed smile and some colour in his face. All the same, it was him, no question about it.

Incredible. But also frustrating, because no matter how much I looked for more info, I just kept getting variations on the same story. A bit about his home life, his interest in taxidermy… No one had been charged over the hit-and-run. Apparently they never found out

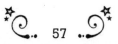

who did it. Was that why he was haunting the school? Was he trying to avenge his death?

I printed out the story. The more I thought about it, the more I wanted to go back there, to see if he would appear to me again. Maybe I could sneak in after school hours. And if he did appear, maybe this time he'd succeed in telling me whatever it was he'd been trying to say before?

Seeing as Maro was feeling a bit bad over the whole Tyburn ghosts thing, maybe I could use that to my advantage; I could ask if she'd let me go out again later on. I sure as hell wasn't going alone, though. I called Ella, but she didn't answer. Then I lost my nerve and hung up. I trusted her, but it would be asking too much. Me, I was suspended already – what more could they do? *She* could get into big trouble. And anyway, I'd have to explain to her about my phantorama, which she'd find really hard to keep secret...argh.

Who else? Sam? But there was the problem of the leg. And Flossie was too young.

Oh well. I'd go alone if I had to.

A bit of luck, for once!

Sam came back from the physio minus the crutches. 'She took them away!' he said, dancing around and

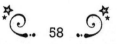

58

promptly stumbling. 'I'm freeee!'

I showed him the printout of the Rat-Man story, and told him my plan for further investigation…well, wild horses weren't going to keep him away.

'Are you sure you can manage it?' I asked.

'*Manage* it?' he said. 'Are you kidding? No way am I missing this!'

'OK, you do realise it's highly unlikely you'll actually see the ghost yourself?' I said.

'Hey, you've got a mystery wants solving. You need me.'

Typical Sam – modest he isn't.

Of course, then Flossie insisted on coming too, not wanting to be left out. So here we were, all three of us, creeping through the bushes along the side of the school's science wing. It was still light, just, but with dark clouds looming murkily overhead. There wasn't a whole lot of time: tonight we were all going out for dinner to celebrate Sam's newfound freedom.

I knew the Friday after-school schedule was just drama club and some music lessons, which would be in a different department – the science wing would be dead quiet. Ha! If you can say that 'dead' means 'quiet', that is…

Sam stumbled, and grabbed onto my arm for support.

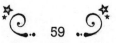

'Careful!' I hissed. 'How's your leg?'

'Not used to taking the weight,' he said. 'Don't worry, I'll be OK.'

'What if we get locked in?' whispered Flossie.

'We won't,' I said. 'At least, we'd better not.'

'Or locked in the broom cupboard by old Grindley, for that matter,' said Sam.

I shot him a sharp look.

'Who?' asked Flossie, eyes like saucers.

'He's the caretaker,' I said. 'Don't take any notice of Sam, Floss. That's just his idea of *humour*.'

Grindley really had locked some kids in the broom cupboard once, to teach them a lesson for being rude to him. I was pretty damn nervous about him myself. Apparently the kids had almost passed out from lack of oxygen…

'Don't worry, Floss, we won't get locked in,' said Sam. 'I know old Grindley's routine from when I've been here for football. He always waits till the after-school clubs finish before he starts locking up.'

'OK,' whispered Flossie, 'but I'm still nervous. What if he does it differently this time?'

'Trust me, I know his routine,' hissed Sam. 'He won't make a separate trip to lock up the labs when he can take care of it all in one go. He's lazy like that.'

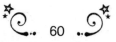

'Sam's right, Floss,' I said. 'Don't worry about Grindley.' I hoped I sounded convincing.

I slipped out of the shrubbery and went up to the science wing entrance. My hand shook as I punched out the entry code, but I didn't panic and forget it, thank god. The door opened, and we went in. It was completely deserted. Sam's shoe made a squeaky noise on the shiny floor and we all winced.

We hurried along the corridor. I peered through the glass panel in the biology-lab door; nope, nobody was in there either. We crept into the gloomy room and got down on the floor, so no one would see us through the window. And we waited.

'OK, now what?' said Sam. 'Do we, like, summon the ghost or something?'

I groaned. 'He's not a genie, you know! No, I guess we just…sit here and wait.'

We waited some more.

I did all I could, concentrating on Rat-Man, imagining him appearing before me now – and tried to stay calm about it all. It helped having Sam and Floss there. I guess it was more of a 'tuning in' than a 'summoning' – although, to be honest, I didn't have much of a clue what I was doing. But it seemed logical that if, like Maro said, you could occupy a different wavelength and tune a ghost

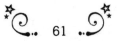

out, then you could also somehow tune them *in*.

But Floss was getting bored and fidgety. She started humming to herself and pulling a cotton wool ball into tiny shreds.

'Stop that!' I hissed.

'Why?'

'It's distracting me!'

'Hang on,' said Sam. 'Did you find that cotton ball on the floor, Floss?'

'Yeah.'

'Uh-oh.'

'What?'

Sam started on about the bin not having been emptied yet, and something about the cleaner coming round...but I wasn't really taking any of it in properly, because just then something started going on in the particles of air around me...a sort of shifting...changing. I couldn't actually see or hear anything...couldn't *feel* anything either. Not literally. I was just aware of a presence emerging, somehow.

And then he was there. Rat-Man was there.

'Aah!' I cried, jerking backwards and knocking a lab stool, *thunk*, to the floor. He was up at the teacher's desk, as solid-looking as any live person. He was holding the rat again in one hand and a scalpel in the other, but his

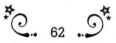

attention was focused on me. His sallow, yellow-toothed face was just as repulsive as before, but somehow not so scary. Maybe because I was prepared this time...or because I'd seen something way more horrible that morning.

'D'you see something?' asked Flossie.

I stood up, not taking my eyes off Rat-Man for a moment. 'Yes...are you sure you can't see him? He seems so...so *real*.'

Flossie shrugged. 'Nope.'

'Me neither,' said Sam.

I was quite proud of myself, because I was really calm and not freaked out. I stepped forward. 'Mr Divine? It is you, isn't it? You used to teach here, right?'

His mouth moved, but again, just like before when his face had appeared in the desk, no sound was coming out.

'What'd he say?' hissed Flossie. Sam shushed her.

'Nothing yet,' I explained. 'But he's trying... Mr Divine? Oh! I wish I could lip-read!' I stepped closer still, almost going cross-eyed as I tried to make out what he was saying.

'Kitteee!' hissed Flossie nervously.

'It's OK, Floss,' Sam told her. 'She knows what she's doing.'

Rat-Man tried again, and this time something did come out – though his voice sounded as if it had been picked up by the wind and tossed through a tunnel and back before it reached me.

'I can hear you!' I said. 'But…can you try again?'

'Um where heanon.'

What? What did that mean?

'Meware eanon,' he repeated.

'Meware…ealon?'

'Meware *eanon*!' he said again, the urgency and frustration showing in his face. The rat dangled helplessly from his fist.

I relayed the words back to Sam and Flossie: 'Meware eanon.'

'Oh my god,' said Sam. 'That sounds like–'

'Beware Eaton!' said Rat-Man at last. Then he fizzled out altogether, as if the effort had all been too much for him.

'No! Don't go!' I called out.

'Shh! Not so loud,' said Sam.

'Oh…he's gone,' I said. 'But oh my god, he was saying: "beware Eaton"!'

Flossie gasped. 'No way. Seriously?'

'Yes…but I wanna know why!' I went towards the desk, trying to reconnect. 'Mr Divine? Mr Divine!'

'Look, we'd better go,' said Sam. 'The cleaner's going to come any minute. We forgot about that.'

I stood my ground. 'No! He might appear again. We need to know more.'

Sam didn't look happy about it, but he let me wait a little longer.

Nothing.

'C'mon, Kit,' said Sam at last. 'We really have to go.'

'No…hang on! The air hasn't settled yet,' I insisted.

'OK, I have no idea what that's supposed to mean,' he said, 'but the cleaner is literally going to walk in any minute. We can come back.'

'OK,' I sighed, and we headed for the door. It wasn't until we were on our way out when Flossie, the last in line, grabbed me by the arm. 'Oh my god, what's that?'

Sam and I turned to look, and there, near the whiteboard, was a marker pen – hovering in midair…

Flossie let out a little yelp, and clung onto me like a limpet.

Sam stood there, his jaw hanging open. 'What the…?'

The pen was moving towards the whiteboard. I rushed over. 'It's him! I knew it – I could still sense a presence. But the energy has changed. Look, he's going to write something!'

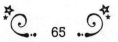

Now the pen hit the whiteboard and slowly, squeakily, words began to appear:

In the cup

Then the pen clattered to the floor. Rat-Man had finally run out of energy completely.

'"In the cup?"' said Sam at last. 'What's that supposed to mean?'

We began searching the lab for cups. 'Beaker?' I said. 'You think he means beaker?' I picked one up from a stack on the counter.

'Cup, cup…what sort of thing we gonna find in a cup, anyway?' asked Flossie, as she peered into one object after another.

We went on searching. Then came the sound of a door opening and closing, out in the hall.

'The cleaner!' gasped Sam. 'Quick, hide – in the cupboard!'

As soon as he said it, we realised at once what Rat-Man had been trying to tell us.

Gallery of Horrors

One cupboard after another turned out to be completely crammed with stuff. There was no way we'd be able to get inside. Meanwhile the cleaner came nearer and nearer with his clanking bucket...

I thought my heart was going to explode. 'They can't *all* be stuffed full! Ah, here's one. This'll have to do.'

It wasn't completely empty but we quickly cleared a space. I winced at the tinkle of a smashed test tube. 'Aah – careful!'

'Come *on*,' urged Sam, as the squeaky footsteps and clanking bucket drew nearer.

We just managed to squeeze ourselves in and slide the door shut before we heard the lab door creak open.

The cleaner got busy with his mop and bucket, singing as he went. *Clunk – slap! Clunk – slap!* 'Oh bay-

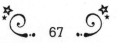

beah! Got to give me all your lovin'!' *Sloop, sloop, clunk –* *slap!* 'Give me all your lovin', yeah…dshhh-sh-sh, weow, weow…' *Clunk – slap!*

I pictured him as I'd seen him so often before, the wires of his MP3 player dangling from his ears. Now, thinking no one could hear him, he was wailing along to it loudly, and making ridiculous guitar-riff noises.

The upside of this was that he clearly hadn't heard the smashing of the test tube. The downside was that I now felt an incredible urge to giggle – the last thing I needed, smooshed in there with Flossie like some sort of packed meat product. I crouched there trembling, my hand clamped hard to my mouth. Was this ironic or what? Here we were, crushed into a cupboard, and we hadn't even been caught by Grindley! At least, not yet. I hoped we wouldn't run out of air, like his victims had.

At last – *clunkity clunk* – the cleaner headed out of the lab, and we all spilled out, stretching our cramped limbs like newly-hatched chicks. We sprawled on the damp floor, taking great gulps of air that reeked of pine cleaning fluid.

'OK,' I gasped at last. 'So now we need to figure out which cupboard Rat-Man was talking about.'

We slid open more cupboard doors, peering inside.

'It's all just the same old stuff,' said Sam.

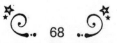

'Hang on,' said Flossie. 'This one won't open.'

Sam and I had a go at tugging; the door wouldn't budge. I knew it was stupid, but I found myself gazing up at the teacher's desk, as if Rat-Man was going to reappear with a key or something. But it was clear that he'd used up his last gram of energy, writing out those words, 'in the cup'. He'd hardly have given up in the middle of a word otherwise.

'It's got to be this one,' said Sam.

'Yeah, it must be. The only thing is, how do we get into it?'

Sam looked at the clock. 'Oh man, you do realise we have about six seconds to figure this out and get out of here before old Grindley comes to lock up?'

I scanned the room like mad, but I was clean out of ideas.

'What are you doing, Floss?' said Sam. I realised that Flossie was shifting the contents of the cupboard next to the locked one.

'I'm going to see if there's any way in back here,' said Flossie, half inside already.

'Way in? How the hell...' Sam and I crouched around the cupboard to see how she was doing. 'What, through a loose panel or something?'

'Uh-huh.'

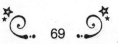

'I dunno,' said Sam, doubtfully. 'These units look pretty sturdy to me. Besides, you've got the radiator behind that part, it's too shallow…'

But Flossie was tiny for her age and flexible like a cat, and she soon proved him wrong; even though the space in front of the radiator wasn't any deeper than my forearm, she got herself squeezed way down inside.

It was taking for ever.

'Hurry up,' muttered Sam under his breath.

'Will you stop going on about the *time*. It's not helping.'

He folded his arms indignantly. 'Fine! Don't listen to me: we've got all the time in the world!'

Of course, annoyingly, he was right to make a fuss. Next thing we knew, there was the sound of footsteps on the gravel outside. Grindley. 'OK, Floss, hurry up in there!' I hissed. Sam pulled a face at me; I glared back.

'Hang on, I got something,' came Flossie's muffled voice.

'What?'

'The back wall of the cupboard here is all sort of bent,' said Flossie.

'Bent?'

'Yeah, it sort of bows out. God, it's hot in here!'

'It's because of the radiator,' Sam said.

'Well, yeah, obviously,' I said.

'No, I mean the bowing out,' explained Sam. 'The back panel has been warped by the heat from the radiator.'

'Oh, of course!' I called inside, 'Floss, can you get your arm through?'

'I…I'm trying, but it's – ow! – it's scraping.'

We listened, getting more and more tense by the minute as she puffed and strained.

'Hey, I got the gap a bit bigger,' she said at last. 'I can get my whole arm in. Now what?'

I tapped the cupboard door. 'OK, the lock's right here, Floss. Can you reach? Maybe there's a way of flicking it open from inside?'

Crunch, crunch, crunch, came the footsteps on the gravel, closer now.

'I don't think those locks on the *school doors* flick open from the inside,' Sam muttered. 'Once we're locked in, that'll be it.'

I thought grimly of the inside of an airless broom cupboard, suffocating…

Then all of a sudden, there was a loud *click!* from inside the cupboard.

'Is that it?' asked Flossie.

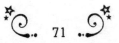

Sam and I dived over and both grabbed at the door. It slid open.

I couldn't believe what I saw.

'Oh my god!' breathed Sam.

'What on earth…?' I trailed off.

Flossie scrambled back out of the cupboard, red-faced and sweaty. Then she saw what was in the cupboard. She gasped. '*What…?*'

The cupboard was full of glass containers, like fish tanks. Inside each one was a dead, stuffed creature. I'd seen similar things in Eaton Antiques and some of the other shops on Portobello Road. But those ones were normal creatures: eagles, owls, rabbits, badgers… These things, on the other hand, were like nothing I'd ever seen.

One had the top half of a normal white rat, but in the middle the fur thinned and turned into fish-scales; the bottom half was a fish tail. Then there was a turkey that was normal in every respect, except that it had two heads. In another tank stood a black cat with little horns poking out of its head, and from its shoulders sprouted wings; with its acid yellow eyes and bared fangs, I'd never seen anything that looked more like a devil in my life. It truly was a gallery of horrors.

But there was no time to gawp; I heard the science wing door slam shut, and now there were footsteps,

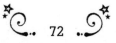

squeaking along the newly cleaned floor of the corridor.

Grindley was inside the building.

We stared at each other, wide-eyed. Normally, he wouldn't have any reason to come inside, but he'd heard something and he was coming to investigate. We were trapped.

'The window!' I hissed. 'Quick!'

A Man and a Van

Flossie was completely shaken up. 'Oh, that was so horrible!' she wailed, as soon as we were clear of the school grounds. 'What *were* those things?'

I tried to comfort her. 'OK, Floss, there there.' I didn't like to admit I was pretty spooked myself. 'They're just—'

'Mer-rat!' Sam burst out, laughing. 'That is *so* cool. Hell turkey! Devil cat!'

'Shut *up*, Sam,' I snapped. 'Can't you see Flossie's freaked out about it?'

'Why? They're just stuffed creatures. If you ask me, it was a lot freakier seeing that marker pen writing on the board all by itself.'

'Yeah well, I was *already* pretty scared by that,' said Flossie. 'And I never knew there were such things as mer-rats.'

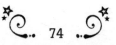

'Oh yeah,' said Sam. 'That's what a water-rat is, didn't you know?'

'Ignore him, Floss,' I said, speeding up to get away from him.

Sam caught up. 'I'm sorry,' he said. 'I'm just a bit hyper, that's all. If you must know, I was kind of freaked out myself.'

'That's OK,' said Flossie, kicking the dirt. She turned to him. 'But they can't be real, those things, can they?'

'No, course not,' said Sam. 'Though I must admit, I quite like the idea of a mer-rat. Or a flying cat from hell.'

I was starting to feel slightly hyper with all the relief as well. Flossie chilled out too, and before long we were giggling. Yeah, even though a ghost had just issued me with a dire warning about my nasty neighbour. Like *that's* a bundle of laughs.

The shadows were stretching across the street as we turned into Portobello Road. It felt good to be surrounded by its familiar sounds and smells. But now I was feeling worried again.

'OK, so we have to beware of Eaton. But what exactly are we meant to do?'

'No idea,' said Sam. 'And what's Mr Divine's connection to him?'

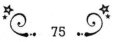

'Yeah, I've been wondering about that, too. We have to find out somehow.'

'And what was Rat-Man trying to tell us by helping us find the monsters in the cupboard?' asked Flossie. She was pretty fixated on those things; I hoped she wouldn't get nightmares.

Sam shrugged. 'Damned if I know.'

'Hold on,' said Flossie. 'If you're saying those monsters aren't real…well, how come they *look* so real?'

I shrugged. 'I s'pose if you can stuff a whole animal, it's just as easy to take part of one, and join it up with bits of other ones.'

'I reckon so,' agreed Sam. 'Probably some weirdos like to have that sort of stuff around the house. Actually, I wouldn't mind a devil cat myself – pity we couldn't have taken it away with us!'

'Ha! Right,' I said, 'Maro would've *loved* that. But what are those things doing locked away in the school, anyway?'

'Well, we know that Rat-Man – sorry, Mr Divine – was a teacher at the school,' said Sam. 'And when you saw his ghost, he was poised to cut open a rat, right?'

'Right.'

'So I guess maybe he's the one that made the monsters.'

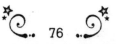

'That would make sense. And – yeah, that piece I read about him on the internet said he was into taxidermy – which is stuffing animals, right? But so what? It still doesn't explain what point he was trying to make about Eaton.'

'You could always go back again tomorrow by yourself,' suggested Flossie, 'and see if he tells you anything else.'

'No way!' I said. 'I can't go back there now. Grindley's probably already onto the police. We just have to hope we weren't caught on the security camera at the gate.'

'Yup,' said Sam, sighing. 'With any luck, he'll just think it's any old vandals.'

'Hey, we're not vandals!' said Flossie.

'Oh no?' said Sam. 'Scrawling on the white board? Smashing scientific instruments? Breaking into a locked cabinet?'

I winced as I thought of the damage. 'Not to mention leaving our fingerprints all over the place. No: we're going to have to figure this out without going back there.'

Darkness fell.

'How far is this place?' I asked Maro, as we trudged

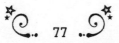

up the hill towards the Harrow Road. 'Seems a long way.'

'Yeah, my leg aches,' added Sam.

'You need the exercise to regain your strength,' said Maro, leading the way. 'And it'll be worth it, trust me. I told you, it's a special place.'

'I'm starving,' complained Flossie. 'Why do we have to go so late?'

'Because they don't open till nine,' explained Maro. 'I told you, this is not your typical high-street restaurant. But you're all going to love it. It's got to be a *special* celebration for my boy!' She ruffled Sam's hair.

I didn't like this part of town, even in the daytime; at night it was even more depressing. There were none of the cute candy-coloured cottages, or the green squares lined with white stucco houses. Instead it was all endless Jenga blocks of grey, streaky concrete…elevated highways…a grim, lonely corner shop with a sinister figure standing outside, watching. I didn't *think* he was a ghost – but I couldn't be sure.

It started to rain. What there could possibly be around here that was so 'special', I couldn't imagine.

'Here we are,' said Maro at last, after we'd come down a nondescript dead-end street where the overground Tube trains rattled noisily past.

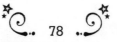

Sam wrinkled his nose. '*Here?*'

Maro knocked on the door of a lonely house at the end, and we waited. Moments later, a letterbox-sized hole swished open, and a pair of eyes appeared. Then the hole swished shut again, and there was the sound of bolts being slid open. The door opened, and a tall black man stood there.

'Hey, Maro, good to see ya!' he said, slapping a huge hand in hers.

Maro introduced us, and we went through to the 'dining room'. Maro was right, it was certainly nothing like any restaurant I'd ever been in before – more like someone's living room. There were only a few tables, none of which matched, and the whole place was done out with such an incredible jumble of mixed-up styles and eras, I didn't know if I was in a 1970s time warp or a Victorian one. One wall was completely covered in old photographs, and the tall man seemed to be in most of them, posing with all sorts of other people. We were practically the only customers.

'Trust me – you'll love it,' said Maro, noticing the look on our faces. 'It's still early.'

'It is?' said Flossie, yawning.

We weren't thrilled that there was no menu either. Everyone just got the same thing – a curry. But then the

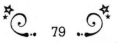

food came and it was surprisingly yum. More people arrived, and the place started to feel warm and cosy and glowing. After dinner a bunch of guys who were from, like, Romania or somewhere, took out some exotic-looking instruments and started playing and singing. Then this pretty Indian girl got up to dance, and after that a few others did as well – including Maro.

Yeah, that's Maro for you.

I've met other people's grandmothers over the years: none of them has ever been like Maro. They do Sudoko puzzles, watch daytime soaps and *Countdown*, ask you what your favourite subject is at school. I can't imagine Maro ever doing any of those things – but then, I can't imagine those other grannies wielding kitchen knives at people, or fixing the plumbing, or throwing themselves around the room to gypsy music, as if they were half their age. When I was little I thought all grandmothers were like Maro; now I know that mine is one in a million. Which is, of course, deeply embarrassing.

We sat there, kind of not knowing where to look while Maro flung her arms around and made strange, jerky movements which made bits of her wobble like jelly under her floaty chiffon blouse.

She beckoned for us to join the dancing. *Nooo!*

'I think I need the loo,' announced Sam.

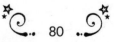

80

'Me too,' I said, jumping up.

'Don't leave me behind,' said Flossie.

We went out into the hallway. 'Where is it?' asked Sam.

'Um…' The stairs were roped off, so we followed the hall down towards the back of the house, where a door was ajar, leading outside. The rain had eased off to a light drizzle; we went out into a dejected-looking back yard, where there was a portaloo.

'Yuck,' I said. 'I hate those things.'

'I'm scared of them,' said Flossie. 'They feel like prison.'

'Well, I'm going in,' said Sam.

He was just about to open the door when we heard a loud squeal of brakes, followed by scuffling noises, thumps and cries.

'What was that?' said Flossie.

'Come on,' said Sam, beckoning us towards the garden fence, near where the sounds were coming from.

We followed him.

'*Oof! Aah! Urgh.*' *Thump, scuffle, thump.* The violent sounds mingled with the jolly gypsy music and hand-clapping coming from the restaurant. But we couldn't see a thing, and the fence was high.

'Let me climb on you,' hissed Sam.

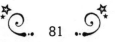

I bent over and he clambered onto my back. His shoes dug in and he was *heavy*. I could hear the pounding of footsteps, the slamming of doors…an engine ignition, the squeal of tyres.

Sam jumped back down. 'Quick!' he hissed, and we followed him back through the house, avoiding the dining room, to the front door. Nobody heard as we slid open the bolts on the front door and slipped outside. I made sure I left the door almost-but-not-quite shut. We stared down the dark, glistening road, but there was nothing to see – we were too late.

We were all out of breath. 'What the hell was that all about?' I gasped.

'Did you see anything?' Flossie asked Sam.

'Well, I…sshhh! Did you hear that?'

We listened.

There was a shuffling noise behind us.

We turned and froze, peering in the direction of the sound, down the darkest recesses of the dead-end alley. More shuffling, and a groan.

'There's someone there!' hissed Flossie.

I could just make out the shape of someone lying on the ground. It *was* a bit freaky, but then I realised: this person wasn't capable of harming us right now, even if they wanted to. I stepped forward.

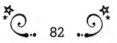

'Hello?' The figure stirred; something black and wet glistened. 'Are you all right?'

'I'm…fine,' came a croaky man's voice.

'Sorry, but you don' t *seem* fine,' said Sam. 'We heard everything.'

I got a glimpse of the man's face as he lifted his head. He had dark, sticky-looking stuff all over his forehead, his nose, his cheek.

Blood.

'Oh!' I reeled back. I couldn't help it. Then I kind of forced myself towards him again, looking anywhere I could except his face. He was in a really bad way. 'We need to get you to hospital,' I said. 'Sam, call an ambulance…and the police!'

'No!' cried the man, now staggering to his feet. 'I'm *fine*. Really.'

'But you–'

'No police! No ambulance,' protested the man gruffly. He leaned forward, now dimly lit by the yellow streetlight. He held his hand over his wound – blood trickled between his fingers. 'Look, just go…it's none of your business. Leave me alone!' And he hobbled away.

We all just stared after him in disbelief. 'Why doesn't he want help?' I said. 'I don't understand…'

'I don't know,' said Sam. 'But I do know one thing. I

saw the van that just drove off, got a glimpse from over the fence. And I recognised it.'

'You did?'

'Yeah. I've seen it loads of times from my bedroom window. It comes and goes from one of those garages in the yard – it's definitely the same van.'

'How on earth d'you know? It was dark and you only saw it for a second.'

'I saw the number plate.'

'Hold on,' I said. 'You *know* the *registration* number?'

'I've had a lot of time on my hands,' explained Sam. 'Believe me, when you're stuck at home with your leg in a cast, you notice things like that. I didn't have time to capture the whole thing as it was driving away, but I did notice the letters at the end, "CLD". It always made me think of the word "cold".'

'OK, but that doesn't mean anything,' I said. 'There must be plenty of vans with registration numbers that end in "CLD".'

'Really filthy white ones with the words "Kev woz ere" written in the dirt, in exactly the same way, in exactly the same place?' asked Sam. 'The tail lights lit up the back just enough for me to see that, too.'

'Ah.'

Just then, Maro came hurrying out of the restaurant.

'*Pethakia!* What the hell are you doing out here?'

'We just…' I began, casting a quick glance at Sam and Floss.

I couldn't tell Maro the truth. She'd only want to go to the police, and the man had been adamant he didn't want that. But my mind was blank – all I could think of was that mess of blood.

'It was getting kind of stuffy in there,' said Sam at last. 'We just wanted some fresh air.'

Maro stood there looking at us, hands on her hips, and for a moment I really wasn't sure she was convinced.

'Well, you're very silly, all of you,' she said. 'Come on, we've got a lift home.'

I heaved a sigh of relief.

I was still pretty hyped up, but the darkness, the quiet and the motion of the car made me practically fall asleep. Flossie and I went to our room, and we just crashed out. So much to talk about…too much. We needed to sleep.

I guessed I'd been asleep for about three hours when I was woken up by a scratching sound. The sky had cleared and there was a full moon. Cold light shone through the window, which was dewy with condensation – our curtain rail had fallen down and Maro hadn't got around to fixing it. I looked over at

Flossie, but she was curled up, motionless.

Scritch, scritch, scri-i-i-itch.

It was coming from across the room, by the fireplace. I sat up and stared. Nothing moved. The moon's reflection shone back at me from the mirror above it.

Scritch, scri-i-i-itch.

A little white rat appeared.

It sat on its haunches, nose twitching, looking this way and that. Then I got that sense again, of a presence emerging – and maybe the rat did too, because it shot like a white streak across the floor and disappeared behind the desk.

I looked over at Flossie again – out like a light. Then the moon's reflection shivered, and the shapes in the mirror slid sideways. They slid in a circular motion, and a white hand pressed itself out of the mirror and into the room.

Rat-Man's hand.

Window Addressing

I'm typing this now, and he's in my room.

Rat-Man. Is. In. My. Room.

And I'm on the computer because if I don't do this I'll scream or something. This is me doing writing, doingwritinganstuffandefinitelynotlookinglalala. I'm sitting sideways so as not to have my back to him, but no way can I look right at him.

Will he talk to me? I don't know if I want him to or not. I mean, I DO want to know more…but if he says something I might just freak out.

Yes…I'm scared.

He's…agitated. Going back and forth – I'm aware of the movement but I can't hear it. Is he looking for the

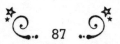

rat? Or something…someONE else? There's a smell…the smell of the science lab.

He's stopped moving now.

I can feel his eyes on me. I'm not going to look up. I'm busy, see? BUSY. I'm not bothered.

Oh god…he's saying something. It's that wind-tunnel voice again, can't make it out. But I'm NOT looking up.

'Gackth le ladth.' That's what it sounds like. And again…the energy is slipping away, I can feel it. The smell, too.

Slipping, going…thank god, he's going.

I'm waiting. Oh – now a squeaky sound. But not like a rat. Like a…a finger on a damp window. He's writing again! OK, I'm gonna look…yes, an invisible finger is writing in the condensation. It says…

CATCH THE RAT

I woke up early the next morning – way too early, considering – to shrieks from the living room.

'He can't do this!' cried Maro. And then she mouthed off in all manner of Greek expletives.

I dragged myself into the living room to investigate. Flossie and Sam had woken up too and they trailed after me.

Maro was leaning out of the window. Outside I could see a man on a ladder, nailing a sign to the wall. It read: 'Acquired by Eaton Antiques Ltd'.

'Take that sign down immediately!' yelled Maro. 'He's not getting us out!'

The man rested his hammer on the ladder and took a piece of paper from the breast pocket of his overalls. 'I'm very sorry, madam, but according to this list–'

'I don't care about your stupid list!' screamed Maro. She reached out, snatched the piece of paper from his hands and tore it up into tiny little pieces that scattered in the breeze. 'Now go away!' She slammed the window down, marched into the kitchen and started clattering around with the coffee pot.

We knew to stay out of Maro's way when she was in this sort of mood. Not that she'd have taken it out on us or anything – she just needed to stew in her juice for a while.

'Conference,' I said, and we all went back into my room.

'This does not look good,' I said.

Flossie looked like she was on the verge of tears. 'I thought Maro was gonna sort it. She promised!'

Sam shook his head. 'I'm not sure there's anything *to*

sort. There's nothing on paper – nothing that counts, at least.'

'Yeah,' I said. 'As far as I can tell, all she's basically planning to do is stay put and say, "We're not leaving. What are you going to do about it?"'

'...And all that's going to do is put off the evil day a little bit longer,' Sam added.

'We need to catch the rat,' I said.

'You what?' said Sam.

I explained all about my night-time visit from Rat-Man, and what he'd written on the window. 'Look,' I said, showing them. 'You can still make out the words.'

'Oh my god!' said Flossie. 'He was right here?'

'Yep. And I wish he'd fill us in properly. It's so frustrating, getting just the odd phrase here and there. But he must be talking about Eaton again.'

'OK, maybe we should tell Maro about this,' said Sam.

'What?'

'Yeah, just about last night's appearance, I mean. We can pretend he gave the "beware Eaton" warning at the same time.'

I thought about it. 'We *could*...but what's she going to do? Go to the police and say, "Hi, I want to report

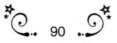

90

this man because a ghost told my granddaughter to beware of him?"'

'No, but she'd know to...I mean...' Sam trailed off. 'Hmm.'

'She already *knows* he's a snake,' I said. 'Unfortunately.'

'If we start talking to her about Rat-Man,' said Flossie, 'I'm worried I might forget and say something that gives the game away about us sneaking into the school yesterday.'

We all agreed we didn't want that. Maro would be furious if she knew; we'd probably be grounded for a week.

'Let's leave it,' said Sam. 'Like Kitty says, there's probably not much point in telling her anyway. One thing's for sure – Rat-Man knows something *really* bad about Eaton, something worse than what we already know. And I'm wondering...' He thought for a moment, then said, 'Let's go into my room. There's something I want to show you.'

We followed him there, and he went over to the window. 'OK, see the garage on the end, the blue one?' he said, pointing down into the courtyard. 'That's where I've seen the van – the one we saw driving off last night after the beating. There's two guys who load and unload

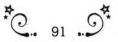

91

stuff. It's always the same guys. What I didn't have a chance to say last night was that they work for Roderick Eaton, I'm sure of it.'

Flossie and I gasped.

'What?' I said. 'How do you know?'

'Well, pretty obvious stuff – I've seen them wheeling antiques back and forth across the courtyard. I don't actually see them going in the back of Eaton Antiques, but it doesn't take a Sherlock Holmes to work out that's probably where they're going. The only other door that opens onto the courtyard is the kitchen of that restaurant.'

'No, no you're right,' I said. 'They must be taking deliveries to and from Eaton. Huh. So…why were they duffing that guy up?'

Sam shrugged. 'Who knows?'

I gazed down at the garage. 'We don't even know for sure if they actually work for Eaton, just because they do a lot of deliveries to the place. Maybe they work for someone he buys from. You ever see them *with* Eaton?'

'Well, no,' said Sam.

'Are they there, like, every day?' asked Flossie. 'Or just now and then?'

'Not every day,' said Sam. 'Maybe a couple of times a week – and always at lunchtime. Actually, today's

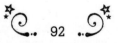

Saturday. I think that might be one of their days.'

Then something struck me. 'Oh my god.'

'What?' said Sam.

'I just thought of something. The hit-and-run incident, five years ago – the one that killed Rat-Man?'

'Oh, you don't think…?' Sam's sentence hung in the air.

'I think the article said it was a white van,' I said. 'But…I'll need to take another look. I know they didn't get a registration number, which is why they never found out who did it.'

'Wow,' said Flossie. 'So Eaton might've killed Rat-Man?'

'Hold on, hold on,' said Sam. 'Let's not get carried away. First things first. Kitty, you double-check that piece about the accident. Then we do a bit of snooping, check that the guys with the van really are working for Eaton.'

'Sam's right, Floss,' I said. 'We mustn't jump to conclusions. I mean, even if those guys do work for Eaton, that still doesn't necessarily mean they were working for him when they went and beat up that man, does it? It could be something they just did themselves, nothing to do with him.'

'I guess,' said Flossie.

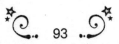

'Then there's the monsters in the cupboard,' said Sam. 'Rat-Man *really* wanted us to know about those – why?'

'I don't know,' I said. 'I mean, they do have stuffed deer heads and things in Eaton Antiques – but those are normal animals.'

'Maybe the monsters were a sort of sideline?' suggested Sam.

Flossie bit her lip. 'Well, whatever's going on, I hope we figure it out *soon*…like, before we get booted out of here. If he's guilty of something major, then maybe he'll go to prison and we won't have to move out after all.'

'Yeah, good point, Floss. That would be amazing. But to be honest, I just want Rat-Man out of my life,' I said. 'He's followed me here, and something tells me he's not going to leave me alone until we find out…whatever it is we're meant to find out. It's one thing *seeing* ghosts, but having them actually *haunt* you is freaky as hell. I'm getting to the bottom of this – whatever it takes.'

Pony and Baloney

I checked the article. Yes, the hit-and-run vehicle had been a white van. That was all the witnesses could say. It was moving too fast. But that was five years ago! What did that really tell us?

Later on Maro went out, and we hung around in Sam's room keeping watch on the courtyard. It was completely empty, despite all the chaos going on round the corner in the market.

Finally, just after noon, we heard the rumble and chug of an approaching van echoing around the courtyard.

Flossie jumped up. 'They're here!'

'Uh-huh,' said Sam, lighting up. 'And the van sounds white and dirty to me.'

'And "CLD" is on the number plate,' said Flossie, at the window. 'Yep – that's the one!'

'Off you go then, Kit,' said Sam. We'd agreed that only one of us was needed for this mission. 'And remember – the more you can observe of them inside the shop, the better.'

'Yup.'

I bolted out of the room and down the stairs.

The van had just pulled up outside the garage when I got down to the alleyway. I dashed into the courtyard and dived behind some big hulking wheelie bins – just in time. A second later I heard the slide and slam of the van doors.

The bins were disgusting and totally reeked of rotting food. I held my nose. After a bit I risked a peek round the side. There were two men, talking to each other in sort of barks and mumbles that I couldn't make out. I got a good look at them before they disappeared behind the van. One was chunky – arms like the big fat Baloney sausage they sold in Nino's Deli down the road. Shaved head. White vest stretching over a barrel-shaped chest. I got a glimpse of his face – hard, and permanently scrunched-up, like a bulldog.

The other bloke had long mousey hair tied back in a ponytail. He was more the wiry type – younger and leaner, but I could tell there was strength in those tattooed arms. Now that I thought about it, I'd seen

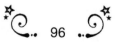

them around before. Both had that sort of chipped and scarred look of guys who'd been in a fair few scraps. Yeah, I could just imagine them beating someone up...

I could hear noises like they were opening up the doors of the van and the garage. I kept my fingers clamped to my nose, hoping this wouldn't take too long.

After a bit I heard wheels trundling on cobblestones. I hid back behind the bin. The van doors slammed shut. Then there were the guys again – Pony and Baloney – coming towards the building, pushing a wardrobe on a trolley and yakking about I don't know what, some random TV show, nothing useful. They passed by the bins, and went in the tradesmen's entrance of Eaton Antiques.

Quiet.

I came out of my hiding place and gratefully inhaled the slightly-less-stinky air. I was convinced it was the same van that Sam had seen in the alley, but just to be sure I took a look round the back of it. Yup, there they were: the words 'Kev woz ere' fingered into the grime on the left rear door. So: no doubt there.

OK, off to Eaton Antiques.

Rounding the corner onto the Portobello Road, I shuddered as I passed the life-size wooden Beefeater

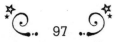

outside the shop. It had a lurid grin that reminded me all too much of Eaton himself – probably the reason he'd bought it, I reckoned. At least I knew I wasn't likely to see him personally. He usually had other people running the place for him.

All the same, this wasn't the kind of place I normally mooched about in, like the indoor market. It was a *proper* Antiques Shop, so proper scary. You just wouldn't go there in a million years 'cause you'd know that some scary person would pounce and say, 'Can I help you?' and you'd be rumbled and have to run away. I could've tried to look like a real customer, but at thirteen, how was I really going to do that? Even if I put on posh clothes I was hardly going to look the part. And seeing as I didn't *have* any posh clothes, that wasn't an option. Instead I had on the usual stuff – you know, baggy T-shirt, shorts, my long socks with different stripes, high-tops with strawberry laces.

But I needn't have worried. It was pretty busy in there, being a Saturday, and there were plenty of other time-wasters – I spotted some Japanese and Italian tourists, all milling about gormlessly. I blended in.

Then I saw Pony and Baloney coming in from the back of the shop, wheeling the wardrobe. No big surprise there; what we still didn't know for sure was

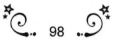

whether Eaton was actually their boss. That was what I needed to find out.

The shop was a big, double-height space with a spiral staircase leading to the upstairs gallery that ran round three sides of the shop. There were creaky floorboards and threadbare rugs, yellow walls crammed with prints, paintings and stuffed animal heads staring out, dead-eyed and dusty. Huge crystal chandeliers dripped icily from the ceiling. It was kind of awesome actually – in a creepy way.

'Vulgar in the extreme!' I heard someone say behind me.

I turned around. There, sitting at a dining table and sipping from bone china cups, were two old ladies. They were wearing rigid high-necked dresses with full skirts that reached the floor, plus dainty little hats with veils on top of curly hairdos. Ghosts – no doubt about it.

'Look, Hilda – all those heavy scrolls and cornices,' the lady went on, as she watched the wardrobe being wheeled in. 'No taste!'

I was relieved. For a minute there I'd thought someone was being rude about *me*. But at the same time it was a shock – I'd been so fixated on my investigation, I'd actually forgotten about my phantorama! And I wasn't used to hearing ghosts talk. I remembered what

Maro had said about Mum, how she'd said that the voices of some ghosts came through loud and clear, and others not at all.

The other old lady – Hilda – pursed her lips and said, 'I agree, Hortense. But it'll sell, just you watch. My word, but I'm quite *beside* myself with boredom in this place!' She wittered on about how all she wanted was a nice home to go to, a bit of peace and quiet, a nice, roaring fire… She stroked the modest-looking dresser beside her and sighed. 'But it's vulgarity that sells, Hortense. No one seems to care for simple, understated elegance.'

'No! You are right, my dear, so very right,' said Hortense. 'And I cannot fathom why nobody seems to want my beloved escritoire,' she added, gazing at an elegant writing desk nearby. 'I wouldn't part with it for the world.'

'Computers,' I said.

The old gals didn't react.

I tried again. 'People don't use traditional writing desks any more.'

A couple stared at me as they walked past.

'…Though I agree with you, Hilda,' Hortense went on. 'Being in this place is so very draining.'

Nope, they really couldn't hear me.

Maybe making ghosts hear me was something I hadn't developed yet. I couldn't tell whether Rat-Man had heard me or not. All I knew was that he'd certainly tried to get *me* to hear *him*. But it was as if there'd been a wall of soundproof glass between us, and occasionally he summoned enough energy to melt a hole in it and say something – in that sucked-through-the-wind way. Then the energy wilted, and the hole closed up again. It wasn't fair – on either of us! And it was really irritating having to listen to ghosts like Hilda and Hortense – who had *nothing* interesting to say – and not at least be able to say something back.

A woman's voice jolted me out of my thoughts. 'Is Mr Eaton in?' She was talking to the man at the till.

'I'm afraid Mr Eaton isn't really in very often,' said the man, a weary-looking guy with a thin grey comb-over who looked intensely busy doing nothing in particular. 'I think he's going to pop in after lunch,' he added. 'Be a couple of hours yet, though.'

'I'll be gone by then,' said the woman. 'What about…'

She went on talking, but I couldn't hear what she was saying, because Hilda and Hortense were making too much noise. 'Over here, for heaven's sake!' they were yelling. 'Buy this! It's lovely!'

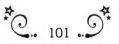

'Sshh!' I hissed at them – which of course was utterly pointless.

The couple glanced back, giving me very funny looks now.

I would have to tune the old biddies out, like Maro had said Mum learned to do – like tuning out a conversation on a train, or blocking out an annoying little sister. Different wavelength: *la la la, can't hear you.* I got nearer to the salesman's desk, and concentrated every last drop of my brainpower on him and the woman he was talking to.

'No, I'm afraid he doesn't come here during the week at all,' said the man.

'Well, when *can* I see him?' the woman demanded sniffily.

The man leaned forward, clasping his hands. '*I* can help you with any queries you might have, I can assure you. Mr Eaton is a very busy man. Were you looking to buy or sell?'

The woman sighed loudly, as if to say *she* was the sort of person used to dealing with the *boss*, thank you very much.

The man cleared his throat and picked up a pen. 'If you give me your details, I can have him call you,' he suggested.

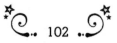

'No, never mind,' said the woman. 'Perhaps you can help me after all…' And then she started describing some sort of cabinet she was looking for.

Boring. And not helpful. Meanwhile Pony and Baloney had parked the wardrobe and looked like they were about to leave.

All the same, I hung around. I glanced back at Hilda and Hortense's little spot – interesting. They were sort of transparent, and their voices faint – though now that I was focusing my attention on them, they were coming back. Maybe Maro was right, I could learn to be good at this. I turned to concentrate on some objects in a display cabinet. Again, the voices faded.

Meanwhile the snooty woman left the shop. As soon as she had gone, Baloney sidled up to the salesman and nodded in her direction. 'That another…*special* client for the boss?' he asked.

'Nah,' said the man, 'just a time-waster. That one he's lunching with is, though. If the boss comes back all puffed up and grinning from ear to ear, we'll know he pulled off the deal.'

A deal? Whoah. Now *this* was interesting.

Baloney nodded and winked at Pony…then he turned his gaze on me. Oops. Time to leave…

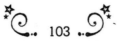

10

Four T K

I pulled out my phone and called Sam. 'OK, seems those guys with the dirty van really are working for Eaton. But there's more…I need you to come out now…bring some money, anything you've got…never mind that it's your savings, we need the cash now! …Tell you later, just come to the shop…no, the next block down, by the pub. We've got some spying to do.'

Sam and Flossie appeared moments later, bobbing through the crowd of shoppers. Sam frowned. 'What do you need my money for?'

'I found out Eaton is having lunch with a "special client",' I said, drawing the quote marks in the air as we headed down Portobello Road. 'The guy in the shop said something about him cutting a deal.'

'What sort of a deal?'

'Dunno, that's what I was hoping to find out.

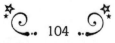

So, we go to the restaurant.'

'What restaurant?'

'Well…I don't exactly know.'

'Kitty! There are around fifty restaurants in the W11 area alone!' (Trust me – he really does speak like this.) 'You mean you have *no idea* which restaurant?'

I flashed him a look. 'Well, I couldn't exactly go up to the guy and *ask*, now, could I?'

'It's probably that one with the squiggly trees out front,' said Flossie suddenly.

'What one's that?' I asked, then I remembered. 'Oh, I know. You mean the one we saw his Jaguar parked outside that time.'

'More than one time,' corrected Flossie. 'I saw it there just last weekend. I remember, because me an' Maro saw him come out, and we ran away.'

'Right,' I said. 'That sounds like a good place to start.'

'What if he sees us?' asked Flossie. 'It's gonna look odd, three kids coming into a posh restaurant by themselves. Plus also as well: he knows us.'

'Yeah, not to mention the *expense*,' Sam pointed out. 'You do realise I was just one pound fifty away from getting a box set of Hitchcock movies?'

'Well, we'll trail in behind some adults or something!' I said. 'What's the worst that can happen? C'mon, we

105

have to give it a try.' I picked up the pace and they followed, eventually.

We found the place quite easily, just a couple of blocks away from Portobello where the tourists don't go and it's all just the local rich people buying croissants and posh toys. And there it was, parked outside: the maroon Jaguar.

'He's here!' cried Flossie.

'Wow. Must be his favourite haunt,' remarked Sam.

I nudged him. 'Oi. Less of that, *brother*.'

'What?'

'Ectoplasm…favourite haunt…'

Sam laughed. 'Oh no! I promise, that time I wasn't joking.'

'Oh yeah?'

'Honest to god!' Sam insisted.

I smoothed down my clothes, but let's face it – this *was* a joke. No way was I going to be able to smarten up. I had my hair in two sloppy bunches, and my long fringe hung halfway down my face, as always. I tightened up the bunches a bit and smoothed my hair to the side – for what it was worth. Flossie did the same. Sam was neat as usual anyway.

'All right,' I said at last. 'Here goes.'

We went in.

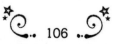

I'd never been in a restaurant like this. It was like something you see in magazines, all smooth muted tones and tasteful lighting. It even smelled expensive. There was a bar area at the front where a few glossy adults lounged in their designer clothes. If Eaton Antiques was scary, then this was scary times ten.

We stood at the front desk, where there was the most gigantic arrangement of flowers. A man appeared, moving towards us as swiftly and silently as a ghost.

'Good afternoon,' he said, looking us up and down. 'May I help you?'

Making sure I was shielded from general view by the floral display, I told myself, *you're the daughter of a famous rock star, you do this sort of thing all the time.* 'Um, table for three, please,' I said. I was quite pleased with how nonchalant I sounded, actually.

'Do you have a reservation?' He was smooth, he was glossy, and he pronounced the last word, 'rezer-VASS-e-ong'. He was terrifying.

'Oh, no, we didn't have time,' I said, trying to make it sound as if I simply had *such* a busy life, details were really just too dull.

'I'm sorry, mademoiselle, but we are fully booked.'

Oh. This I wasn't prepared for. I risked a peek around the edge of the branches of almond blossom.

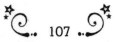

Beyond the swanky bar area was a dining room that did, unfortunately, look very full. 'Oh, well, um…'

'That's OK,' said Sam. I noticed he'd gone rather pale, having just consulted a menu he'd picked up from the desk. 'We only came for…for tea,' he added, quickly putting the menu back.

'I'm afraid we don't do afternoon teas here, sir,' said the man. *We don't serve riff-raff, now go away*, he might as well have said.

'Dessert!' I said. 'Could we please just have a dessert? We won't stay long. My…*our* daddy comes here all the time, you know.'

A subtle lifting of the eyebrow. 'Oh? I beg your pardon. Perhaps I know him, then?'

'He's…Jack Grey,' I said, giving the first rock star's name that popped into my head.

'Really?' said the man. 'Well, of course I know who he is, but–'

'*Please*,' said Flossie, stepping forward. She treated him to her famous big brown-eyed gaze. 'All we want is to have some dessert or pudding or sweet. We won't be any trouble.'

Mr Smooth didn't exactly melt, but he did seem to defrost a little around the edges. 'We're fully booked, Miss Grey,' he insisted. 'However, you may have your

dessert in the lounge area. Follow me.'

My heart sank. What had I been thinking? Did I actually believe that we'd not only get a table, but also be seated close enough to Roderick Eaton to eavesdrop on his conversation? While also somehow being able to conceal ourselves from him? I hadn't thought it through. Typical me – straight in, without thinking. Still, what else were we going to do? I followed the man miserably.

We were seated at a low table at the far end of the small bar and given dessert menus. A partition separated us off from the main dining room.

Sam looked at the menu anxiously. 'We haven't got enough money – there isn't anything here for less than seven quid and all I've got is eleven-fifty.'

'Well, we'll share one then,' I said.

We ordered something I'd never heard of from the menu that did at least have the word 'chocolate' in it – then, because the waiter seemed very tetchy about us ordering just one thing between the three of us, we asked for a lemonade as well.

I took a peek around the side of the partition – and quickly sat back down. 'Oh my god, I see him.'

'Eaton? Who's he with?' asked Sam.

'Skinny guy…long hair…shades…kind of spooky-looking actually.'

'OK, but you're sure he's *not* a spook,' said Sam.

I gave him a withering look. 'Yes, Sam, I'm sure.' I took another peek, just in time to catch Eaton as he left the table and began to cross the room – in the other direction, thankfully. 'Oh! I think he's going to the loo,' I hissed. 'Sam, follow him in there!'

'What? Why?'

'Just go – you never know. Only try not to let him see you. Go on!'

Sam sighed and got up.

When he was gone, I took another look at Eaton's lunch companion. He wore a black satin shirt, tight black pinstripe jacket, silver necklaces and rings...all very goth. But expensive goth, I reckoned. Then Eaton came back, followed by Sam.

Sam sat next to me. There was a sort-of smile on his face.

'Well?'

'OK, I admit it,' he said, 'this probably was a worthwhile way to spend my savings.'

Flossie and I leaned forward. 'Yeah?'

'I went in and dived straight into a cubicle,' Sam began. 'He didn't notice me. He was talking on his phone – all excited, he was. Said he'd clinched the deal – something about "four T K", whatever that means.

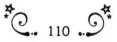

And that he'd be picking "it" up – whatever "it" is – from someone called Alvaro on Wednesday at five o'clock...' He fell silent as the waiter brought us our Chocolate Something and the lemonade. I waited impatiently.

Finally, the waiter left again.

'Brilliant, Sam! Well done. I bet this is something illegal!' I dug my spoon into the Chocolate Something. 'Now, if we can just find out what "it" and "four TK" are, and who this "Alvaro" is...' I trailed off, noticing that Sam was just staring grimly at the dish, not having touched his spoon. 'What's the matter?'

'I don't know, Kitty,' he said. 'We could be getting onto some dodgy ground here.'

'What do you mean?'

'Well, like you say, I *do* watch a lot of those detective movies. And if I've learned anything from them, it's this – when you've got people making these private deals involving lots of cash, there are always people getting bumped off somewhere along the way.'

'In the *movies*, Sam,' I reminded him.

'No, look, think of *The Maltese Falcon*–'

'I never understood that movie,' I said. 'Gave up after about the first ten minutes, couldn't make out *what* was going on.'

'Never mind the *movies*,' hissed Flossie. 'I think Sam's

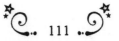

111

got a point. Look, we saw a guy get beaten up! Eaton might be behind that – probably *is* behind it. And who knows? He might've had them *kill* other people, or murder them even, like Mr Divine. Plus also, his *murdered ghost* told you to' – she lowered her voice even further – ' "beware Eaton!" '

They both looked at me.

'Well?' said Sam.

I dropped my spoon onto the plate. 'So what are we doing here then? You knew this was about some big deal before we even came here!'

'I know,' said Sam. 'But…it only hit me just now, in the loo.'

'Great,' I said, trying hard to keep my voice down. 'That's just great.' I took a deep breath. 'Look, do you have any idea…?' I trailed off. I was going to say, did he have any idea what it felt like to be stalked by a ghost? But, ha! Pointless question or what? 'All right. Well, I don't know about you,' I said at last, 'but I'm going to get to the bottom of this, one way or another. We can't give up now. We just can't.'

Phoney Arrangement

Oh god. Here he is again.

OK, I'm not going to freak out this time. Here we go...that chemical smell, the squeaks and scuffles of the rat. Right, Rat-Man, I'm ready! Come on! I'm going to talk to you.

3.45AM

OK, that didn't work. He just keeps saying the same things – 'Beware Eaton' and 'Catch the Rat', in that same wind-tunnel voice – but he doesn't hear me when I try to ask him something.

So now I'm going to tune him out, like I did with Hilda and Hortense. I'm going back to bed.

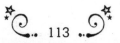

Right, that didn't work either. All that happens is he gets louder – and there's nothing else to distract myself with. Even with my head under the pillow, it's no use. He soon stopped saying actual words – after that it was all groans and stuff. Just NOISE. And Flossie, meanwhile, slept blissfully through the whole thing.

I just had to wait until he ran out of energy...gone now. Back to sle-e-e-ep...

The alarm went off.

'Come on, get up!' nagged Flossie.

I knew without looking that it was only seven-thirty – way too early.

'Go away!' I mumbled into the pillow.

'But Kitty, it's a school day!' insisted Flossie.

'For *you*.'

'No, for you too!'

I ignored her and zizzed off, then was woken again by Maro plonking the laundry basket on my bed. 'Come on, *Kitaki-mou*, time to get up. You're going to have lessons with Sam this morning, like we said.'

'Urgh. But I've hardly slept!' I could have explained about Rat-Man's visits, but what could she do about it

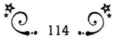

114

anyway? She'd only get even more worked up than she already was.

More plonking, as Maro sorted the laundry into piles on my bed.

'Do you have to do that here?' I groaned.

'Yes,' said Maro. 'You *could* just get out of the bed… *Flosaki-mou*, did you finish your homework?'

'Yeah,' said Flossie, 'I just have to print it out.'

I heard the electronic groan of the computer waking, and suddenly realised I hadn't shut it down properly last night. I looked up to see Flossie staring at my ghost blog on the screen. I'd been so out of it, I hadn't even signed out. She looked at me, and I winced dramatically.

Flossie quickly collapsed the blog window. 'Actually, I think you should let Kitty have a lie-in, Maro. I remember now, she had…some really bad dreams. Didn't you, Kitty?'

Thanks, Floss! I winked at her. 'Yeah. About those Tyburn ghosts. Horrible…'

Maro looked up at me from her laundry piles, her face full of guilt again. 'All right, *Kitaki-mou*, you can have another hour.'

I wandered into the kitchen, yawning. Didn't feel much better after the extra hour, to be honest. But Maro had

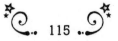

got me up just before she left to take Flossie to school, and this time there was no negotiating; she made sure Sam would see to that.

I put the kettle on.

'You making tea?' he asked.

'Yeah.'

'Do me one, will you?'

I yawned again loudly. 'All right.'

'You OK? Maro said you had a rough night, and I wondered–'

'Yeah – Rat-Man.'

'Did he say anything new?'

I stuck some teabags into mugs. 'Nope. Urgh. I thought maybe he was giving me a break, seeing as we're…you know, on the case. He didn't bother me on Saturday night at all. Mind you, now that we're *dithering*, and might not follow things *through*…'

'God, Kitty, I feel bad,' said Sam.

Yes, I thought, *you're meant to.*

'You really think he's not going to leave you alone until we get to the bottom of this, huh?' he asked.

'I get that impression, yes,' I said. I couldn't help sounding sarcastic. 'What would be great is if he could just tell me exactly *why* we need to beware Eaton, and *what* to do about it, but…' I trailed off.

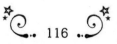

As I dumped the teabags in the bin, I noticed Maro's mobile phone on the counter. She'd left it behind, charging up. For some reason that my fuggy brain couldn't quite connect up yet, this seemed like something interesting and useful…

'What is it?' asked Sam.

The words were swirling around my brain again, like they'd been doing for half the weekend:

Alvaro. It. Four T K.

Who was Alvaro? What was the thing Eaton would be picking up from him? What did 'four T K' mean?

Alvaro… I picked up Maro's phone and stared at it, thinking. I hit the 'names' button, bringing up her list of contacts.

'Sam,' I said.

'Yes?'

'What if we got hold of Eaton's phone somehow, without his knowing – just for a moment? Maybe we could get some more info on this Alvaro, like his surname. Maybe even his address.'

'And *how* do you propose to get hold of Eaton's phone, exactly?' said Sam.

'Erm…get him round here again?'

Sam rolled his eyes. 'OK, first of all, I don't know how you think you're going to do that, after what

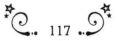

happened the other day. And secondly…hmm, let me see…' He stroked his chin in mock thoughtfulness. 'Oh yeah – *you're out of your tiny mind.*'

'I'm not!'

'Kitty, it's dangerous! "Beware Eaton" – remember?'

'I know! That's exactly why we need to find out what happened to Rat-Man – before he *haunts me to death.* Anyway, aren't you *furious* with Eaton? You're not seriously going to just sit around and let him boot us out of our home, are you?'

'Well, Maro–'

'Well, Maro nothing! She's just putting a brave face on things. Anyway, what's the worst that could happen? It's not as if Eaton does his *own* beating up or anything.'

'Oh, that's OK then,' said Sam sarcastically.

'OK, you know what? I'm doing this anyway.' I started punching keys on Maro's phone. 'Either you're in or you're out, but I'm doing it.'

'What are you going to say? "Sorry I waved that knife at you. I was only kidding! Come over for a chat, you're a good laugh?"'

'I'm going to say she has a business proposal. You heard him, suggesting she might like to buy him out, which he *knows* she can't…'

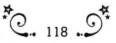

Sam was silent for a moment, watching as I composed the text message.

'Hang on, hang on,' he said at last. 'All right, I'm in. But if you're going to do this, you've got to do it right, or else Eaton'll smell a rat…er, as they say. Like, don't use any abbreviations. You know how she insists on doing full words, even though she doesn't know how to use predictive text.'

'Yeah, I know…blimey, this phone is like, from the Ice Age or something. Why doesn't she get a new one?'

'Because she's sixty-five years old,' said Sam. 'Same reason she takes about ten minutes to write a text message.'

'OK, how's this?' I said, showing Sam the message display.

I have had another think, and I have a busness proposal that I think will interest you. Please can you come round at exactly 3pm today to discuss?

'Oh, big giveaway, that "exactly",' said Sam. 'Delete that. You put it because you need him to come right when she's out picking up Flossie, but think about it – she wouldn't say that, would she? Oh, and you mis-spelled

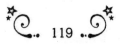

"business". Also, he's a busy guy, remember? Add "or tomorrow", give him a bit more leeway. Put "Mr Eaton" on the front as well. I think she always does that, like she's writing a letter or something.'

'OK, done.' It was good to have Sam working with me again. I made the changes, then hit send.

I put the phone back down on the counter and we stared at it, waiting.

Nothing.

I poured myself some cereal. I was just adding some milk, when Maro's phone burst into tune, along with that loud buzzing noise you get from phones sitting on hard surfaces. I jumped, jerking my hand and spilling milk onto the table. 'Rats!' I grabbed the phone and hit view. It was a message from Eaton:

Be there 3 today

'Yes!' I quickly erased both sent and received messages and put the phone back on the counter where Maro had left it.

'OK, we're in business. Let's talk tactics.'

At five past three that afternoon the door buzzer went. I dived into my hiding place behind one of the double

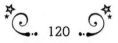

doors leading to the living room. From there I had a good view of the kitchen through the crack between the door and its frame. Part of the plan was for Sam to pretend he had the flu. I watched him as, dressed in pyjama bottoms and sloppy sweatshirt and carrying a fistful of tissues, he went over and pressed the intercom.

'Hello?'

The buzzy, crackly voice came back: 'Hello…Mrs Slade?' Even with the distortion, I could tell it was Eaton.

'No, but she'll be here any minute,' said Sam. He gave me the thumbs-up as he buzzed Eaton in.

A moment later there he was, coming through the door. My stomach did a flip; suddenly I was scared again. I realised how much had changed since the last time he was here; back then he'd just been plain nasty. Now, he might actually be dangerous. Sam was right…oh, why was Sam always right! And now I couldn't get the words 'beware Eaton' and the image of the beaten-up man's bloody face out of my mind.

Well, no going back now. Eaton was here.

I watched his bloated red face twitch with impatience. 'Well, well now. Grandma on her way, then, is she? Haven't got a lot of time, y'know, lots to do, lots to do.'

Sam, unlike me, seemed totally cool now. Go figure.

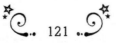

He gave a loud sniff. 'Yeah, she's just cubbing,' he said.

'Mmm. Well, as long as she's not wielding a kitchen knife this time,' said Eaton.

Right, like you didn't deserve that, I thought.

Sam gave a shouty fake sneeze into his tissue. 'Sorry,' he said. 'I've got the flu.'

Eaton backed off a little. 'Right…well. You go on back to bed, then. I'll just wait here.'

'Thank you,' said Sam. 'I think I'd better. You can bake yourself some tea if you like…um, and sorry if it's a bit hot in here.'

I took a peek at Eaton. He loosened his tie. *Good.*

'We had to turn the heating up,' Sam explained, shivering. 'I'b got terrible chills.'

'All right, well, off you go,' said Eaton.

'OK…bye.' Sam went to his room.

Meanwhile I watched as Eaton took off his jacket and put it over the back of a chair. Excellent – this was exactly what he was meant to do, and the real reason we'd turned up the heating. Sam had noticed last time Eaton was here that he kept his phone in his jacket pocket.

Now all we needed was to get Eaton away from the kitchen for a while. We had a plan for that, and it had been my idea. Knowing that the window in Sam's

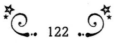

bedroom was jammed shut, I suggested Sam ask for Eaton's help with it. Never mind that we had the heat whacked up; feverish people were always cold one minute, hot the next. He needed fresh air, didn't he? So Eaton would spend some minutes yanking on the thing, giving me the chance to–

'*Eathnon! Meware Eathnon!*' bellowed Rat-Man, suddenly appearing beside me. The chemical smell was there too, and the rats – yes, that's rats *plural* – running all over the floor.

No! Shut up!

I couldn't say anything. And even if I could, it wouldn't do any good. But I needed to hear what was going on in the mortal world. *Tune him out, tune him out…*

I thought I heard Sam call…yes, must have done, as Eaton moved off into the hall. All of a sudden I felt properly nauseous. The nickname 'Eaton Alive' now felt like a sick joke. What if he was onto us? What if he knew he'd been rumbled…that we knew too much about his terrible secrets? He might cause an 'accident'… I pictured a pair of leather gloves being pulled on, the window somehow being flung open…then a sharp shove, and…*no, stop it!*

I was letting Rat-Man freak me out. Eaton didn't

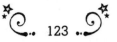

know anything about my encounters with Mr Divine's ghost, or that we'd witnessed the beating. There was no reason for him to hurt us! I had to calm down. Sam would be OK.

Just as we'd planned, I picked up my shoes and backpack and crept across the kitchen floor in my socks. I reached for the inside pocket of Eaton's jacket. Oh, but if I could only get Rat-Man to shut up…and all those rats! All over the kitchen floor…*eek, eek, eek!*

I *had* to tune them out. Only while I could hear voices from Sam's room – he'd promised to keep Eaton talking – would I know that Eaton wasn't about to appear again. And now I had their voices to focus on, I found I *could* screen Rat-Man out…a little. Enough to hear something, at least. I was suddenly grateful for Eaton's booming voice.

I stared at the phone, which was completely different from my own. I hit the middle button, and the phone instructed:

now press *

But my hands were shaking, and I kept failing to hit the two buttons quickly enough to get the keypad unlocked. Finally I got it – but then the phone beeped!

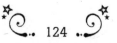

God. I only hoped it couldn't be heard from the bedroom.

After that, finding my way to the address book was easy. And 'Alvaro' was only fifth on the list. But no sooner had his contact information appeared on the screen than I heard Sam announce loudly, 'Oh, thank you!', which we'd agreed was the signal for me to get out of sight. *No!* I needed more time!

Fingers shaking, I scrolled down in the hope that Eaton had Alvaro's street address on his phone…yes! Here it was. I memorised it as best I could. Then I hopped around, getting into my shoes while at the same time exiting the address book. I dropped the phone back into Eaton's jacket pocket. Then I picked up my backpack and dived for the front door, just getting it open and closed as Eaton reappeared from the hall, followed by Sam.

'Oh, hello,' I said, acting all surprised. Rat-Man, thankfully, was gone by now.

'Ah, Kitty,' said Eaton. 'Is your Grandmamma with you?'

'No. I just got back from school.' I dropped my backpack on the floor.

Eaton sighed, glanced at his watch, then went to the kitchen and reached for his phone.

Oh my god! I didn't lock the keypad! I suddenly thought.

Too late, I realised I was staring at Eaton.

Eaton stared back. 'Is something the matter?'

'Oh, no…nothing,' I said. *It doesn't matter, it doesn't matter…*

Eaton frowned slightly at his phone, then said, 'Well, I can't hang around much longer. I'll call Grandma to see if she's nearly here.' And then he went ahead and called Maro.

Oh no. This *did* matter. I shot a glance at Sam. Damn! Why hadn't we thought of that? Of course he would call her. And now we were done for. Eaton would figure out what was going on, and…Eaton Alive…

The seconds crawled by. If Maro was in a noisy playground or a busy street, maybe she wouldn't hear it.

Please don't pick up, please don't pick up…

Maro didn't pick up.

'Hmm, no answer,' said Eaton, pocketing the phone and putting his jacket on. 'Waste of time! Look, just have her call me, all right? I happened to be passing just now, but really, I need to get going.'

'Yes, of course!' I said, trying not to sound too ecstatic.

The moment he was out of the door, I grabbed the

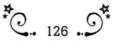

shopping list pad and scrawled out the address from memory. 'There!'

I showed it to Sam:

Basement, 114 Jones Road, W12 something

'Fantastic!' said Sam. 'Well done, Kit. We did it!'

An Invented Cat

As soon as Floss was back from school, we all got together in Sam's room.

'W12 is the postcode for Shepherd's Bush,' I said, completely psyched now. 'I've been there before. You get the 94 bus, it's not far.'

But Sam had gone all serious and thoughtful again. Not a good sign. 'Ye-e-eah,' he said, staring at the note.

I sighed. 'OK, now what?'

'Don't get me wrong,' said Sam. 'I'm really pleased we got this and everything. But…well, now that we've *got* the address, what exactly are we supposed to *do* with it? Hang around outside and watch, while Eaton pays a visit?'

'That was bothering me too,' Flossie chipped in, 'but I thought you had it all figured out.'

'And even if we somehow managed to do that

without being seen,' added Sam, 'what would we learn from it? Precisely squat.'

'Well, of course we don't hang around outside!' I said. 'We go into the flat.'

'We go *into* the flat,' Sam repeated slowly. 'We get ourselves invited into the home of someone who doesn't know us from a hole in the ground…and then presumably get him to let us hide there while Eaton pays him a visit. OK, help me out here.'

'Well, that's what we're here to discuss!' I said. 'But yeah, that's the idea. We need to be able to eavesdrop.'

'*All* of us?' asked Flossie, looking nervous.

I thought for a minute. 'I dunno, maybe we don't *all* go. One of us should probably hang back, in case of emergencies…'

The look on their faces was not encouraging.

'I know what you're thinking,' I added quickly, 'but it's not gonna be dangerous if none of them knows we're there!'

Flossie shrugged. 'That's true. But…'

Sam just frowned, letting that 'but' dangle in the air between us. BUT…

I wasn't going to be put off. 'So,' I said. 'Any ideas on how we get in without Alvaro knowing?'

'Oh, that's easy,' said Sam sarcastically. 'We just get

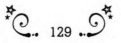

him to leave his front door open.'

I ignored his tone. 'Exactly!' I clicked my fingers. 'And how do we do that?'

'Pretend we're collecting for charity?' suggested Flossie. 'Like, ask if he's got any old clothes to give away, so he'd have to go and look in the bedroom?'

Sam rolled his eyes. 'There are so many things wrong with that idea, I don't know where to *start*.'

Flossie looked injured.

I flashed my brother a look. 'Well, I'd say that was pretty good thinking, *actually*.'

Sam sighed. 'OK. Number one, charity people don't go round asking people to rummage in their cupboards for stuff. They deliver bags for people to fill and leave out for collection. Believe me, I've spent enough time hanging around at home to know these things. Number two, charity people always show ID cards. Number three, they're always adults.'

I only half heard. My mind was focused on that open front door. 'Get him to look for something…' I muttered. 'Flossie's onto an idea, though…hey – how about a cat?'

'A cat?' echoed Sam.

'Yeah, you know – pretend we live down the road and we've lost our cat. People do that, don't they? They go round asking their neighbours.'

'Yeah,' agreed Flossie. ''Cause cats hide away when they're lost and scared, and then they get accidentally locked in cupboards and things. Remember Maro's friend's cat, that was found in a garden shed?'

'And this is a basement flat,' I said. 'So it'll have a garden, or some sort of outside space, right? Somewhere the cat might've got into.'

'Yeah!' said Flossie, warming to the theme. 'Aah – *poor* kitty!'

'It's not a *real* cat, Floss,' I reminded her.

'Hmm…' said Sam. 'So we ring on the doorbell, he answers…we know he'll be in…then we ask about the cat…'

'Yes,' I said. 'And then, when he goes and looks, we slip inside and hide…no – hang on: we don't *all* hide. *One* of us asks about the cat. Then, when Alvaro goes looking for it, the others go in and hide. There – that's what we do.'

Sam folded his arms. 'Then how do we get out?'

'Well…' I collected my thoughts. 'Um, well, that shouldn't be so hard, right? Once you're *in* someone's place, it's easy to get *out*.'

'Ha! As long as you're not seen,' added Sam.

I sighed again. OK, so he had a point! But sometimes

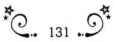

I wished he could just go for it, take the chance, not worry about things so much. 'Do you actually *want* to find out what Roderick Eaton's up to, Sam?'

'*I* do!' said Flossie. 'We can go, just you and me, Kitty. You be the one to ask about the cat and I'll be the one to hide. I'm good at hiding!'

'No way are you going by yourselves,' said Sam. 'It isn't safe!'

'So you'll come along and protect us then?' I asked.

Sam sighed. 'Yeah, I s'pose so.'

I gave him a squeeze. 'Yay! Sam-the-man. I knew you wouldn't let us down.'

Alvaro's

'I'm hungry,' said Flossie, as we took our seats on the top of the double-decker bus after school.

No, you're nervous, I thought. I knew what she was like – nerves always made her hungry. Complete opposite of most people, but that's Flossie for you. I pulled a cereal bar and a small bottle of water from my pocket. 'Here you are. This'll keep you going. And don't worry, Floss – I told you, if anything goes wrong I've got my phone and I'll be straight onto the police.'

It was Wednesday, the day Flossie usually had her ballet lesson, so Maro wouldn't be expecting her home for some time. Same went for me, as it was normal for me to collect Floss. And Sam had told Maro he'd come along too. Maro had been surprised. 'But you never go,' she'd said. So Sam explained, 'Well, I couldn't walk before! Now I like to get out as much as I can.' Which

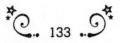

Maro seemed to buy – no more questions asked.

And now here we were, on our way to Shepherd's Bush, and the home – or office, or whatever – of Alvaro. In silence. Well, except Flossie, who was munching loudly.

I went over the plan in my head. What we couldn't predict was how Alvaro would behave; we had no idea what sort of person he was. What did we know about him? Exactly two things:

1. He had a foreign-sounding name
2. He was apparently the person who supplied whatever dodgy thing it was that Eaton was selling to Mr Goth-Man from the restaurant.

Not a hell of a lot. And yet we were about to sneak into his place, right when the deal would be going down!

It was risky, but what choice did we have? Forget about the whole thing? Not an option. Just report to the police what we knew so far? Well, what good would that do? We still had no proof that Eaton had anything to do with the beating we'd witnessed, no 'hard evidence', as Sam would say. No: we had part of the jigsaw puzzle in place, but there were still plenty of pieces missing – it didn't connect up. We might be able to get Pony and

Baloney into trouble, but not Eaton. As for the deal involving Alvaro and Goth-Man, for all we knew so far, it was all perfectly legal. No way would the police be bothered if we said, 'Oh, there's this businessman and he's got some private deal with this bloke that we think might be a bit dodgy.'

So it was up to us – we were on our own.

It was drizzling when we got off the bus at Shepherd's Bush Green, all grey and heavy and tired. Even the 'green' was murky and full of rubbish. I'd checked out where Jones Road was, and by the time we got to Alvaro's house it was twelve minutes past four. There was still the best part of an hour to go until Eaton's appointment.

Number 114 was right at the end of a dead-end street. The houses were the typical London Victorian sort, all tall and crammed together and mostly white or white-ish. They started out looking quite smart but as you went along the street they got more and more shabby. Number 114 had apparently once been painted white too, but that was obviously a long time ago; now it was covered in that blackish grime you get from all the pollution. And years of rain had crumbled away bits of it and added a layer of green moss. There was pigeon poo all over the windows, and the railings along the

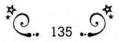

135

front were falling apart with rust.

'Blimey,' I said. 'He's not well-off, is he?'

'Uh-uh.' Flossie wrinkled her nose at the state of the basement, which looked about as inviting as a rubbish dump. One good thing – the curtains (tobacco-coloured and falling apart) were drawn, so it was easy for us to stay out of sight. Plus Alvaro was playing some music – loud, thumping, brassy sounds that reminded me of the Notting Hill Carnival. That was also good as he wasn't likely to hear us.

We went down the crumbling, slippery steps to the basement level. One problem: no bins to hide behind. That had sort of been the plan, but we didn't reckon on them being up at street level. No matter: there was other junk, a stack of wood that looked like bits of broken furniture, leaning against the wall. As I'd volunteered to be the one to ask about the 'missing cat', Flossie and Sam were the ones who hid, squeezed behind the wood stack. I helped shift some of the bits of wood, making sure they were well hidden.

Then I took a deep breath, went over and rang the doorbell.

And waited.

After a moment, the door opened just a little way. The music spilled out. A small man with darkish skin and a straggly little beard hung back in the shadows – Alvaro, presumably. He gave me a wary, suspicious look.

'Hi,' I said loudly. I thought maybe if I sounded confident, I might be able to feel it. 'I'm sorry to bother you, but I live down the cat…I mean, the *road*, and our cat's gone missing, and I wondered if–'

'I havven seen no cat,' interrupted Alvaro. He moved to close the door.

No! Once he closed the door, that would be *it*. I stepped forward. '*Please*,' I begged. 'None of the neighbours are answering…this has happened before, and she was found right around here. Please?' I treated him to the special big-eyed sad-person look that was my little sister's speciality, hoping I stood a chance of getting the full Flossie Slade melt-your-heart effect.

Alvaro paused, then pulled the door only about an inch wider. 'You can look in the back yard if you wan', but only for a minute. I have to go out.'

Well, that was a lie, I thought – probably because he wanted to get rid of me before Eaton came. But hey, I was just relieved to be let in at all. I went all gushy. 'Oh, thank you, you're ever so kind'. Blah, blah.

'But I haven' seen no cat,' Alvaro reminded me.

It was so dark in the flat that it took my eyes a while to adjust. The place smelled of a whole bunch of unsavoury things, like rotten potatoes, dirty linen, sweaty leather… There was something like the Rat-Man stink as well: the sharp, chemical science-lab smell. For a moment I wondered if Rat-Man himself was about to appear, but he didn't.

God, the flat was grotty! A scuzzy pit of a place. As my eyes adjusted, I found myself wondering what on earth Eaton could possibly be getting from this guy that was so important. There were just a couple of lamps giving off a dim, yellowish light. There was a big old sofa against one wall that had a whole load of manky cushions and blankets on it. I reckoned it probably doubled as his bed. Piles of dusty books and old vinyl records were stacked around the edges of the room, and what was left of Alvaro's lunch sat on a low table in front of a clunky old TV. It all made me feel vaguely clammy and nauseous, but I needed to keep my wits about me. My job was to check the place out for cupboard space. I glanced around – yup, there were a couple of doors that looked as if they might belong to cupboards.

I followed Alvaro down the hall, past a tiny kitchen and into the heavily overgrown back garden. I suddenly realised I hadn't actually thought of a name for the cat. My brain went completely blank, so I just went with 'Flossie'.

I started yelling, 'Flossie! Flooo–seee!' like a complete lunatic, getting my ankles soaked in the long wet grass. Alvaro hovered behind me like a shadow. And then I remembered something else – I wasn't actually supposed to come out here myself! I'd been so panicked and nervous, I'd forgotten what the plan was: I was supposed to wait by the front door while *Alvaro* looked for the cat. That was the whole point! I needed to be *inside*, so I could find a hiding place, then let Sam and Flossie in.

Oh wow, I thought, *that was dumb.* I turned to Alvaro. 'Um, actually, Flossie often goes into other people's houses, like in their laundry cupboards and stuff. She likes the warmth, you see. I don't suppose I…?'

'I haven' *seen* no cat!' He was getting quite fed up now.

I had to persist. 'All the same. Since I'm here…?'

Alvaro just stood aside and gestured with exaggerated patience for me to return indoors.

'Thank you,' I said, heading back inside. I tried smiling at him, but he was still stony-faced. Clearly I was not achieving the Flossie Slade melt-your-heart effect.

Worse still, he followed me every step of the way. *No, no!* He wasn't meant to do this!

He opened up a broom cupboard. I didn't really want to lean in. It felt as if at any moment he might shove me inside and lock the door, just like Grindley had done with those kids…

My mouth was as dry as paper. 'Flossie?' I croaked, tilting forward ever so slightly.

Alvaro hovered behind.

The cupboard was crammed with stuff, but there was some space. Better still, it was right opposite the front door. Fine, but unless I actually got the others in, I'd have achieved nothing.

'Um…are there any other cupboards?' I asked.

'No,' replied Alvaro firmly – even though I was sure I'd seen another door that looked like it could be one.

Now what? I couldn't leave. I had to find a way of sticking around longer. 'Could…could I just try one more time out the back?' I dared to ask. 'Flossie might have heard me before? But been quite far away?'

Alvaro sighed. 'Just for a minute. I told you, I gotta go out.'

'Oh please don't mind me,' I said. 'You carry on with…getting ready or whatever.' I went back out, relieved that this time he didn't follow me, but went into the kitchen instead.

I called a few more times. Figuring that maybe Alvaro would be occupying himself with something or other by now, I risked creeping back into the flat. I sneaked past the kitchen. He had his back to me, and thanks to the carnival music, he didn't hear me either. I hurried over to the front door and opened it oh-so-gently. Sam and Flossie were at the ready, and dived straight into the flat, then into the broom cupboard that I hastily opened up for them.

Then, leaving the cupboard door almost-but-not-quite shut, I headed back towards the garden – but I didn't get far before Alvaro appeared at the kitchen door.

'Oh! Hi,' I said, hoping he'd think I'd only just got in from the garden. 'Well, no luck,' I added, as I returned to the front door for the second time. 'But thanks for letting me try.'

'OK, bye,' said Alvaro, following close behind.

Then I was out in the street again…alone this time. Which felt very weird, and not at all good. In fact, very bad. Walking away, I felt like I'd been cut in two. Up until now, we'd been a team…now we were separate. My brother and sister were shut away in a cupboard in that stinky hovel of a flat, to face…who knew what? Suddenly, I felt guilty for getting them involved in this

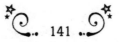

whole plan. What if it went horribly wrong? I'd never forgive myself.

But it was too late to do anything about it.

I would just have to wait.

Waiting

It was ages yet till Eaton was due to arrive – almost half an hour.

I walked around the block, then down to the main road. At least it had stopped drizzling – the sky had brightened up a bit. I wandered around the Turkish supermarket to distract myself. It was full of exotic fruit and vegetables, and the shelves were stacked with packets of stuff with names like *Sari Leblebi* and *Besni Uzumu.*

I wondered what on earth you were meant to do with half of them. There was some Greek and Middle Eastern stuff too, so I played a game with myself: see how many things could also be found in Maro's cupboards.

Maro. I was meant to call her. I left the shop and pulled out my phone. It went to voicemail. 'Hi...sorry,

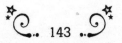

the lesson was delayed,' I lied. 'So they're running over time. We'll be back in about half an hour.' Just as well she wasn't answering – it was easier to lie to the voicemail. Maybe she'd gone to her salsa class or something – good.

Suddenly I was gripped with nerves all over again. I checked the time. It was still only ten to five. I walked back up to the dead-end bit of Jones Road, where there was a sad little patch of green, a couple of flowerbeds and more rubbish. There was a splintery bench beside a tree – a good spot, I decided, well hidden from the road. I sat down and waited.

At five o'clock on the dot, the familiar maroon Jaguar, together with a certain filthy white van, drew up outside number 114. Roderick Eaton and entourage had arrived.

I held my breath. *Here we go*, I thought. *Please let Sam and Flossie be OK.*

The visit only lasted about ten minutes. Then Eaton came out, talking on his phone, followed by Pony and Baloney. Baloney was carrying a tea chest, which he loaded into the van. They got into their vehicles, then the Jaguar turned around and drove back down Jones Road, followed by the van and its slogan, 'Kev woz ere'.

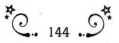

What was inside that tea chest? Would Sam and Flossie know by now? I realised I didn't even care. I just wanted to know they were OK.

All I could do was wait. They were bound to come out soon, surely? The cupboard was right opposite the front door – all they had to do was slip out as soon as Alvaro left the room. But as the hazy sun dipped down below the council flats across the way, there was still no sign of them.

What was taking so long?

I started imagining things…like Alvaro opening the closet door and finding them…Eaton seeing them too, then instructing Pony and Baloney to…to what? Beat them up, like they did with the man in the alleyway? No, surely not. But he might tie them up or something…

I shuddered as an icy chill ran through me. At first I thought it was just because I was anxious or because the sun had gone in…then I noticed the old geezer sitting next to me. He hadn't been there before; he'd just appeared out of nowhere. A ghost.

'Have ye seen my dog, by any chance?' he asked.

I so did not need this right now. 'No,' I said.

He was pretty old, with a silver-stubbled chin and stains all down his rumpled black suit and moth-eaten tweed coat.

'I fell asleep,' he went on, 'and now I wake up and he's gone!'

'No, you didn't just fall asleep,' I said gently. 'You died.'

'He's black and white, blind in one eye,' he rambled on, oblivious.

His puffy red face was punctured by a pair of the saddest eyes I'd ever seen. Suddenly I felt a huge wave of sympathy. Poor old man – he had the look of a homeless person. He'd probably died right here on this bench, with his dog sitting there pining...for a time. Then the dog would have moved on. And here was the spirit of the old man, still wondering where his dog had got to... maybe years later. Wondering, helpless...

'I'm sorry,' I found myself saying, and I could feel the tears welling up. 'I wish I could help, really I do...'

'He's a bit of a one for the ladies,' the man was going on, still not hearing, 'so he does tend to go off now and again. But he's been gone an awful long time now, so he has...'

I thought about Sam and Floss. I wanted so badly for them to appear now. Why weren't they coming out? It was more than I could bear. The tears welled up in my eyes and I began to sob, not caring any more if I drew attention to myself. The old tramp didn't react.

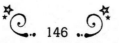

Instead he just faded away.

Suddenly, I heard a sharp noise: the sound of a door shutting.

And it was nearby…as near as…could it be?

Yes it was – basement flat, number 114.

But my heart sank as just one figure appeared – and it wasn't Sam or Flossie. It was Alvaro.

The Locked Door

I called Sam on his mobile straight away.

He answered quickly.

'Sam!' I cried. 'Are you OK?'

'Yeah, we're fine. But we're locked in.'

'Oh no! He locked you in the cupboard?'

'No, silly, we're locked inside the *flat*. He's locked the back door and there's no key in it. And he's locked the front door from the outside. But we're not ready to leave yet anyway.'

'You *what*?'

'This is the perfect time to have a snoop!' said Sam. 'We hardly heard a thing, they went off into some other room. But as they were leaving they were talking about finding a buyer for "the next one"…hang on…what?'

I heard some muffled talking, then Sam spoke to me again. 'Flossie's found the key to the back door! It

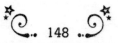

was in a kitchen drawer. Hey, can you get in round the back? Shouldn't be too hard, as it's the last house in the street.'

I ignored the beeping on the line that told me another caller was trying to get through. 'But how do you know Alvaro hasn't just nipped down the road for a pint of milk?'

Beep, beep. 'We heard him talking on the phone as he was leaving, said he'd "be there in twenty minutes". Well, if it takes him twenty minutes to get wherever it is he's going, even if he turns around and comes right back, that's at least forty minutes, isn't it?'

'OK! I'll be right there.' I glanced at my phone. It was Maro trying to get through. I felt terrible about it, but I switched the phone off. *Just for now,* I told myself. Just a quick snoop, then I'd call her back.

I went round the back of the house. The fence was old and faded but there were no gaps for me to squeeze through. And it was *tall.* There was nothing for it but to climb over. I glanced around, then jumped up. 'Ow!' I fell back down, scraping myself. I'd have to get higher than that. I tried again, and again.

Eventually after about five tries, I got a firm grip on the top of the fence. I walked my way up the side and threw myself over. Then I was back in the deep damp

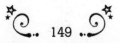

grass, and in no time I was at the back door, reunited with Sam and Flossie.

'Thank god you're all right!' I gasped, as soon as I was inside. 'It was horrible, waiting out there. When I saw that van, I couldn't stop thinking about the man who was beaten up.'

Sam stretched. 'Yeah, well, we're OK. Just cramped, that's all…urgh! I'm going to be stiff for days!'

'I thought I was gonna suffocate in there!' added Flossie. 'And I don't like the smell of this place.'

'Me neither,' I said.

'What *is* that smell?' asked Sam.

'I dunno…anyway, tell me what happened!'

'Like I said, they went off into another room,' said Sam.

'Yeah,' added Flossie. ''Cause we could hear them quite clearly at first, and then they sort of wandered off and it was all muffled after that.'

I looked around. 'What other room?'

'That's what we're going to find out,' said Sam. He opened the first door on the right – the one opposite the kitchen. That was the bathroom. The next one wouldn't open. 'It's locked.'

'Must be the one they went into,' I said.

'Yup, looks like it,' sighed Sam, running his hands

over the door. 'And no doubt he has the key on him.'

'Well, he had that spare back-door key, didn't he?' said Flossie. 'Maybe he has another one for this door too.'

'He might…' I said.

We went into the kitchen. There was a whacking great pot on the stove, and two more on the counter. 'Wow, he must cook for a lot of people,' I said. 'Who'd have thought it?' I was surprised. Everything else about the place seemed to scream 'loner'.

We searched the drawers, but found nothing.

'OK, maybe he keeps the key somewhere else. Let's split up and search.'

We spread out to different corners of the flat and peered into every drawer, every shelf, every nook and cranny. Things were looking pretty hopeless, when Flossie picked up a small pot filled with dusty dried flowers. As she did so, something metallic rattled inside. She pulled out the flowers, reached in and…yes! A set of keys.

'Brilliant, Floss!' I took the keys and tried out each one in turn. None of them worked.

'One of them has to work,' said Sam. 'Try again.'

'Oh-*kay*…' The keys jangled in my trembling hands, but this time I felt one of them engage. There was a click,

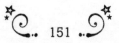

and the door opened. I turned on the light and we went in.

The stench hit me straight away. I clamped my hand to my nose. 'Urgh! So this is where that smell comes from!'

Sam and Flossie covered their noses as well.

'What *is* it?' said Sam.

'I don't know,' I said, 'but it *stinks*.'

The room had no windows – it looked like some sort of workshop. Two walls were lined with workbenches. There was a stack of horizontal racks on one of them, like the ones they use in the art department at school for drying paintings. Part of the bench was where Alvaro worked at whatever he did – there was a swivel chair with a jacket hung over the back of it, a whole bunch of different tools, and some big needles and thread. Leaning over the workspace were an angle-poise lamp and a magnifying glass on a stand. Assorted bits of stuff were hung on hooks above the workstation.

I went to take a closer look. 'This looks like…like leather.'

'Yeah, there's leather over here, too,' said Sam, standing beside the drying racks. 'And look at this,' he added, pointing to some big bottles of brown liquid. He read the labels. 'Tannic acid.' He opened a bottle, took

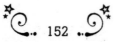

a sniff, and recoiled. 'Ew! That's nasty.'

We had a sniff.

'Gross!' said Flossie, wrinkling her nose.

Sam picked up one of the pieces of leather and sniffed it. 'I think he uses the acid to treat these skins.'

Skins...the word sent a shiver through me. What *kind* of skins?

'Hey, maybe he's a shoemaker,' suggested Flossie.

I looked at her. '*Shoes?*'

Flossie shrugged. 'Maybe bags...'

'They'd have to be one hell of a pair of shoes or bag,' said Sam. 'Do you realise just how excited Eaton was about his "big deal"? I can't imagine all that was over some girls' accessories.'

I pulled a plastic bag out of a drawer under the workstation. 'Look at this – hair. And it looks...it looks...' I couldn't quite bring myself to say the word 'human'. 'This is no shoemaker.'

'I know what I think,' said Sam.

'What?'

'He's a taxidermist. Like your man in the biology lab, Rat-Man. That's what links the three of them. It's why Rat-Man wanted you to know about those monsters in the cupboard. He was trying to tell you something about Eaton, something to do with those.'

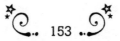

'Maybe,' I said. 'But hang on…where are all the animals, then? I mean, say he was making a mer-rat, he'd use half a rat and half a fish, wouldn't he? There's no evidence that I can see of that sort of thing. And what would he need all the leather and hair for?'

'Hmm…' Sam gazed around. 'You have a point.'

'Maybe he's creating made-up monsters,' suggested Flossie.

I didn't answer. I was too busy searching for more evidence. 'Eaton talked about finding a buyer for the "next one",' said Sam. 'Whatever the "next one" is, it should be here…'

'Look, tea chests,' I said, noticing some large wooden boxes beside the door. 'Whatever Pony and Baloney took away was in one of these.'

'Ah!' Sam went over to look at them. The one nearest to the door had a label on it showing a date. 'Second of March,' he read. 'That's, like, a week ago.'

'The date he finished making it, you think?'

The lid was just resting on top of the box. I lifted it off.

It was full of straw. Sam and I both reached in and began pulling out handfuls, throwing it on the floor. And that was when we saw it.

Nestled deep in the straw was a tiny head.

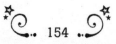

Amazonians

'Aargh!' Flossie cried out, lurching back. 'Oh, that is horrible!'

I clung onto Sam. 'Oh…my…god. What *is* that? Is it real?'

It was only about the size of a grapefruit, but apart from that it was exactly like an adult human head. The skin was kind of shiny and dark. The eyes were shut and the broad nose and mouth jutted forward. The head had long black locks of hair coiled neatly on either side, decorated with strings of colourful feathers, and the lips were sewn together with long, thick threads. It was like some sort of horror-baby, all aged and wizened – like a troll, slumbering away there in its nest. But I felt like it might wake up any minute, staring at me with luminous green eyes…

'It…it *looks* real,' said Sam, forcing himself to move in

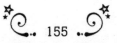

for a closer look. 'In fact…I think I know what this is. I've seen these before in the Science Museum. Shrunken heads.'

'What?' I said. 'Real…shrunken…*human heads*?'

'Eurgh!' exclaimed Flossie. 'That's possible?'

'Yes, it is,' said Sam. 'There's this Amazonian tribe; they'd cut off their enemies' heads, then use this special technique for removing the skull and shrinking…um… what's left.'

I suddenly felt ill. 'Amazonian, did you say?'

'Uh-huh.'

'As in, South American?'

'You know of an Amazon river anywhere else?'

My head began to swim. 'Oh my god…Alvaro. You didn't see him, but…he kind of looks and sounds South American…'

'And that was South American-y music he was playing,' said Flossie.

We all looked at each other.

'No, hang on, this is something the tribes *used* to do, *ages* ago,' said Sam. 'They don't do it any more.'

I looked at the horror troll head, then at Sam. 'None of them?'

His face was pale as chalk. 'Um…'

'OK, this is really creeping me out now,' I said, and

to make things even worse for myself I had to go and look back at Alvaro's workstation, didn't I? Those knives for slicing open a man's skull, those needles for sewing up the lips. Just what kind of skins *had* we seen? And now I thought again about the large pots in the kitchen, large enough to contain a whole head...

I steadied myself on the stack of tea chests. 'What *is* Eaton involved with?'

'Does this mean he's *killing* people?' asked Flossie. 'You s'pose he told his men to kill that man in the alleyway?'

Sam's white face was now glistening with sweat. 'Wait...not so fast! There has to be some rational explanation for all this.'

There was a click, followed by a humming sound. We all jumped. Then I realised it was coming from a small fridge in the corner that none of us had noticed before.

We all stared at it.

'OK,' I said. 'Who's brave enough to look in there?'

Sam cleared his throat. 'Uh...yeah. That might just tell us what we need to know.' He didn't move a millimetre though.

'I'm not doing it,' declared Flossie.

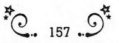

I felt as if my legs would give way if I even tried to move.

'OK, I'll do it,' said Sam at last.

He walked over and opened the door. Icy air spilled out. 'It's not a fridge, it's a freezer.'

Slightly less freaked out at the sight of the neat row of drawers, Flossie and I went to have a look.

Sam reached in, grabbed the top drawer, and pulled…

What I saw inside was worse than I could have imagined. 'Aargh!' we all cried. Quickly, Sam rammed the drawer shut and closed the freezer door.

But the image of what I'd just seen wouldn't go away. Encased in frosty plastic, with an ear and black hair clearly visible was…a severed head.

'Let's get the hell out of here!' said Sam.

We bolted out of the room, not bothering to repack the straw in the tea chest. Sam fumbled with the key in the lock…and then we heard the front door slam.

Alvaro was back.

We made a dash for the back door, but it was too late – he'd seen us.

'Hey!' cried Alvaro, as he came thundering towards us.

And he wasn't alone – another, larger man was with

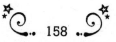

him. I'd just managed to get Flossie out through the door when I heard a scuffle and a cry from Sam behind me. He'd been caught by Alvaro! The keys fell to the floor. In another moment, the larger man was holding me and Flossie by the arms, one in either hand.

'You again!' Alvaro yelled at me. 'What the hell's this all about, huh?' His anger completely distorted his face; there were flecks of spittle on his hairy chin, and his mouth was pulled into an ugly grimace, showing a mouthful of very bad teeth.

'N-nothing,' I protested, 'it was just a game.'

Severed heads…

'A dare!' I went on. 'We didn't mean any harm…'

…knives, cooking pots… Oh, god!

'We were just mucking about. Oh, please let us go!'

'What have you been stealing?' demanded Alvaro, shoving his free hand first into Sam's pockets, then mine and Flossie's. Floss didn't have a phone, but he took mine and Sam's. I felt a little shudder of panic.

'I told you, we haven't stolen anything,' I insisted. 'We weren't even going to.'

Alvaro picked up the keys from the floor and shook them in Sam's face, making him flinch. 'I know what you've been up to!' he yelled. 'You've been in there, haven't you!' He pointed to the workroom.

Sam shook his head madly. 'N-no, I haven't. Honest. I–'

'Don't lie to me!' shrieked Alvaro, his eyes ablaze. 'Who put you up to this, huh? It was *him*, wasn't it?'

'Who?' asked Sam.

'You know very well who!' snapped Alvaro. 'Mr Eaton, right? *Am I right?*'

'That scumbag,' muttered Alvaro's friend.

'Mr Eaton?' I said. 'But we thought you were on *his* side!'

'Me?' Alvaro's mouth twisted into a sneer. 'I hate him! All the time I work, work, work. He makes more and more money, but I get next to nothing. Now he stoops to a new low, eh? Stealing my work – and sending *children* to do it!'

'No, no, honest!' I protested. 'I promise we're nothing to do with him.'

'Yeah, we hate him too!' added Flossie.

I could feel the grip on my arm relax slightly.

'We were actually trying to find out what he's up to, 'cause we know he had someone beaten up, and he's booting us out of our home, and–'

'Whoah, whoah,' said Alvaro. 'What's this? Beat up who? Booting you out – why?'

I was so surprised, I didn't know what to say for a

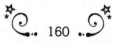

moment. *He doesn't know about the beating?* I thought. *But what about the killings…the severed heads…*

'Actually, we only *think* he's connected to a beating,' said Sam. 'We don't know for sure–'

'Yeah, but we have good reason to think it,' I added. 'Plus, we live above his shop, and he plans to expand and take our place over–'

'OK,' said Alvaro. 'So you don' live down the road, then.'

'Er, no,' I said, averting my eyes.

'And of course there ain' no cat,' added Alvaro.

But I noticed he'd calmed down a bit, which was a relief. He didn't seem to care much about our little scam. All the same…well, I didn't know what to make of him. Because if Alvaro wasn't on Eaton's side, then what exactly was going on with the head in the freezer, and the shrunken head we'd found in the tea chest? Eaton had to be one very sick man – not only did he have his men kill his enemies, he liked to keep their preserved heads as trophies. But no, he didn't keep them, did he? He *sold* them. Why?

It didn't make sense.

'Alvaro?' I said at last, feeling bold now.

'Oh, you know my name too, huh?'

'How many people has Roderick Eaton had killed?'

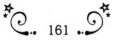

Big Deal

Alvaro and his friend looked at each other. Then they burst out laughing.

'How many people has he had *killed*, did you say?'

I felt my face go all hot. I was really confused now.

Alvaro let go of Sam completely, reached into his pocket for a pack of cigarettes and lit one up. He took a deep drag. 'Tell me, what's your name?'

'Kitty.'

'Tell me, Kitty, what makes you think Mr Eaton is having people killed?'

I didn't know what to say. I mean, I couldn't exactly say, 'Only that we know you're working for him, and there's a severed head in your freezer!'

'Well, I…' I looked to Sam and Flossie for help, but they seemed just as lost for words.

Alvaro took another drag on his cigarette, and blew

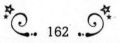

out a thin stream of smoke. Still staring us with a faint smile on his face, he pushed open the door to his workroom. He stepped aside and peered around the door.

'Ah. I thought so. And this…' He reached down and picked up the shrunken head from the tea chest. Its locks and feathered strands hung down below it, spilling bits of straw. 'Do you know what this is?'

'Yes, sir,' said Sam. 'It's a shrunken head.'

'Wrong,' said Alvaro.

What…?

Suddenly a phone started ringing – it was Sam's ringtone. My eye darted over to where it was, in Alvaro's pocket.

Alvaro didn't move. 'Mama wondering where you are, huh?'

'It'll be Maro, our gran,' I said. 'And yes, she probably is wondering where we are.'

Alvaro nodded. 'Uh-huh.'

We all just stood there as the phone rang on. Try as I might, I couldn't take my eyes off the revolting troll-like head dangling from Alvaro's hand.

The ringing stopped.

'OK,' said Alvaro at last. 'I'll cut a deal with you. I'll tell you what this really is–' he raised the hand holding

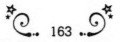

the head, 'if you agree not to tell a soul about it. In return, I will not report you to the police for breaking and entering. I won't even tell your gran.'

'Deal,' I said.

Alvaro handed back our phones. 'You can call. Make up anything you like, just don't say where you really are.'

Sam sent Maro a quick text, then shoved the phone in his pocket.

Alvaro put the troll-head on the coffee table, its long, witchy locks spread out around it. He patted his friend on the back. 'This is Javier,' he told us. 'He just got here from my country – Colombia. First time here.' Alvaro turned to speak to Javier. 'Things are not usually this crazy here in London, my friend.'

'Ha! They are in Colombia,' said Javier.

Alvaro turned back to me. 'You live with your grandmother,' he said. 'So your mother, what happen to her?'

'She was killed in a car crash when we were very little,' I told him. 'We never knew our dad.'

'I'm sorry to hear that,' said Alvaro. 'You want to know what happen to my family? My mother, my wife, my children, all murdered in front of me.'

We all gasped.

Alvaro shrugged. 'Was over twenty years ago –

a very bad time in my country, much fighting. You try to support the right people, and…well, anyway, after that I had to leave. I tell you this so you understand how desperate the situation was. I was very lucky to get here, to London. But was not easy to find work, you know? I can't do building work, I have a bad back. There was not much else. In my country I was, uh…taxidermist especialist? I made these.' He picked up the head again. 'You know about shrunken heads – impressive. But this is not a genuine shrunken human head. It is a fake. I am the best there is at making fake shrunken heads.'

'He is,' agreed Javier. 'The best.'

'You mean…you don't actually use human heads?' I asked.

'No,' said Alvaro. He took a large book off one of the shelves and opened it to a page with a big colour photo. 'This is a real *tsantsa*, as they are called,' he said. 'It is a real human head, and it is about a hundred years old.' He turned to Sam. 'You know how they were made?'

'I just know they took the…uh, skull out somehow,' said Sam.

'That's right,' said Alvaro. 'Is how come they got so small. Was the Jivaro tribesmen of Ecuador did this to the heads of their enemies. After they took out the skull,

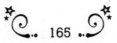

they sewed shut the eyes and removed the fat. Then the flesh was boiled, tanned, dried and…how you say, shaped, moulded. And they sewed the lips together.'

'And…*why?*' asked Flossie.

'They believed that in this way, they could take control over the spirit of the enemy, make it serve them, and not try to avenge their death. Anyway,' he said, shutting the book. 'The point is, real *tsantsas* are very rare. You won't see nowhere, maybe the museum only. You see one any place else, is gonna be a fake, for sure. And mine are good fakes. I use not human heads but heads of monkeys or *perezas*, um, sloths. Or sometimes just using animal skins, but this is harder to make to look good.'

So that would explain all those pieces of leather in the workshop, I thought. But it still didn't explain the human head in the freezer…

I couldn't help wondering if Alvaro was just cleverly covering his tracks. Maybe the heads he was working with really *were* human, and he knew the only thing he could do in the situation was to convince us they were fakes. It would make sense for him to do that, I reckoned, only he didn't know we'd seen inside the freezer. If I was right, then things could turn very ugly indeed if he knew about that…

'…learned some secrets directly from an elder Jivaro tribesman, when I was travelling in Ecuador,' Alvaro was saying.

I hardly heard him. I couldn't take my mind off that head. The frosted grey-black hair…the ear poking out…

'…this is why my work is so in demand,' Alvaro went on. 'Very few people have these techniques…' He paused. 'Something is troubling you, Kitty. What is it?'

'Oh…nothing.'

Alvaro just stood there, looking at me, spooking me out. Then he did the same to Sam and Flossie. He drew a breath, like he was about to say something – then didn't. Finally, he said, 'Let's go into my workshop, shall we? You show me exactly what you looked at.'

Oh no…

We went in.

I was reminded of one of Maro's sayings, about 'the elephant in the room'. The elephant in the room was something terrible or embarrassing that everyone knows about, but nobody wants to mention – here we were, all Not Mentioning the severed head in the freezer.

I hung around near the workstation. 'Well, of course we looked around…h-here,' I muttered. But my body language gave me away. Too late, I realised I'd already glanced over at the freezer.

Alvaro noticed. 'You looked in the freezer.'

Sam, Floss and I all glanced at each other.

'Yeah, OK, that means you did,' said Alvaro.

Oh god, I thought. *Now we're finished.*

But I wasn't prepared for what Alvaro said next. 'I have contacts at zoos in England,' he added, as if that was some sort of explanation. 'This is kind of against the rules, but when an ape dies–'

'An *ape*?' I repeated.

'Yes,' said Alvaro. 'Like I say, I use them instead of human heads, because obviously–'

'Oh! And…they're not killed, they just…'

'That's right; I get them after they die of natural causes. Look, remember I told you this is secret, so–'

'We won't say anything to anyone!' promised Flossie. 'Is that what we saw, then? An ape's head?'

'A chimp, to be precise,' said Alvaro. He opened the drawer again, and we looked inside. I could see now how we had mistaken it for human. The inside of the clear plastic bag was all iced up, so that some of the front of the face was hidden. But when Alvaro picked up the package, you could see the heavy brow and chimp-shaped mouth quite clearly. And the ear was obviously larger than a man's. I guess we'd been too shocked to notice.

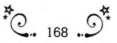

Alvaro put the head back and shut the freezer. 'It's good to get a chimp or a gorilla, but often I have to use a sloth, a monkey…depends what I can get.'

'OK!' I cried. Suddenly I felt quite crazy with relief. 'Good, good…excellent!'

Flossie was, too. She flung her arms around me and burst into tears. 'Oohh, I was so scared!'

'We thought it was human,' Sam explained. Typically, *he* was was all calm and collected. 'We didn't really look properly.'

A sudden, sharp laugh came from Javier. We all looked at him.

'Sorry,' he said, 'but you have to see, is very funny. They thought it was…and you…ha ha ha!'

Alvaro was amused too – but he saw the look on our faces. 'OK, you had a bad shock. Come with me.' We followed him into the kitchen, where he poured us some juice. 'I still wonder, though,' he said, as he took out some coffee. 'Why did you sneak into my flat? What did you hope to find out about Mr Eaton by doing this?'

I gratefully took the glass he handed me and sipped the cool, sweet juice. 'Well, we found out he'd pulled off this big deal,' I explained. 'We had a feeling it was something dodgy, so we wanted to get to the bottom of it.'

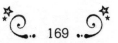

169

Alvaro poured coffee grounds into a little pot on the stove. 'A big deal, huh? Well, I guess you gonna have to keep looking. No big deals around here!'

Once again, we were speechless.

Alvaro looked up and frowned.

'But the head,' I said. 'The fake *tsantsa* you just made for him. We sort of thought *that* was the big deal.'

He laughed again. 'No, no…you make a mistake, Kitty. This is no big deal! Not for a man like him. For me, is all I have, and he keep most of the money for himself anyway. But a big deal? No way. You know, they are good fakes, but…ha! They are still fakes–'

'No, hang on!' Sam interrupted. 'I heard it all clear as day. He was really excited and he phoned someone up, just when he'd clinched the deal – those were his words – and said he'd be picking "it" up from Alvaro at five on Wednesday.'

'Yes, and then we did some more investigating and got your address,' I added. 'It was definitely this deal he was talking about.'

'But we never did find out what that "four TK" was,' Flossie pointed out.

'Four TK?' repeated Alvaro.

'Yes,' said Sam. 'That phone call I was telling you about – he said something about "four TK". I'd forgotten

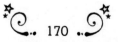

about it until now. Do you know what he meant?'

Alvaro and Javier looked at each other.

'Jeee-zuss!' remarked Javier. 'Forty K? That man is taking you for a *long* ride, if that's what he's making here.'

Alvaro dropped his spoon, scattering coffee grounds everywhere. 'No. It can't be…'

'What?' I was still having a hard time making sense of this.

'Mr Eaton is pretending my fake *tsantsas* are the real thing,' said Alvaro, staring into space, suddenly deathly pale. 'And getting the prices to match – forty K is *forty thousand pounds*.'

Muizak

'We should tell the police,' said Sam.

'No! No police!' snapped Alvaro. He was pacing up and down, wringing his hands.

'Maro, then,' I suggested. 'She'll know what to do.'

'*I'll* deal with this,' insisted Alvaro. 'Is my problem. You kids, you just go now.'

'No, it's not just your problem!' cried Flossie. She was trembling now, her big brown eyes filling with tears. 'We're gonna lose our home, and Kitty's being–'

'I'm worried about how our gran's going to take it,' I butted in. Best to keep the whole Rat-Man thing quiet, I reckoned. It would only sound nuts to Alvaro. I put my arm around Floss, who was a blubbering mess.

Thinking about Rat-Man got me going, though – no way was I ready to just drop this whole thing, not now! I felt anger rise inside me, and next thing I knew, I was

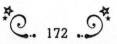

yelling at Alvaro. 'We can't just forget about it, you know! We witnessed a beating by Eaton's guys, plus we have reason to believe...look, we think someone was killed as well. *Please*. Eaton needs to be stopped!'

Alvaro looked taken aback.

Then Javier spoke to him in Spanish, and he seemed just as wound up as I was, hands waving about all over the place. Good, he was on our side.

Sam moved in. 'At least talk to Maro,' he said. 'It's not like you'd get in trouble with the police yourself.'

'No?' said Alvaro.

'Really,' said Sam. 'I've watched enough detective movies to know that the police need all the help they can get from people in situations like yours. They'll be grateful for the information.'

'All right,' said Alvaro eventually. 'I guess your grandmother have a right to know about this.'

'Forty thousand pounds,' I said, as we rode the bus back to Notting Hill. 'Forty *thousand* pounds! What else would you get for that? A house?'

'Ha ha! You'd be lucky,' said Alvaro.

'A Jaguar, like the one Eaton drives?'

'Probably.'

Forty thousand pounds... And there were people

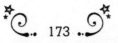

173

who'd pay all that money for a horrible little munchkin head! Crazy world…

I still couldn't get over the relief. The situation was nothing like as horror-movie as it had seemed. But there was still the question of exactly what happened to Rat-Man. Because if all this wasn't about Eaton having people bumped off, then why was he run over? That was no accident – and Rat-Man knew it.

And the monsters were the clue…

Well, if someone was willing to pay forty thousand pounds for a fake *tsantsa*, they'd probably pay a lot for those monsters, too. If Eaton had been using Rat-Man the same way he was using Alvaro, and Rat-Man was onto him, about to report him…that would be a motive, wouldn't it?

No wonder Rat-Man had unfinished business.

'*O vromoskilos!*' cried Maro, when we told her what we'd discovered. 'So *that's* where all the money is coming from! The dirty dog…oh, if we can get him locked up for this, it would be *fantasticos*. We wouldn't have to move out! But…*how* did you say you discovered this?'

'From this man Alvaro, who's the dad of this girl at my school that you don't know,' said Flossie.

I cringed at the clumsy way she tried to deliver the

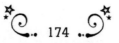

174

story we'd all agreed on. I wondered how much of it Maro was going to believe. I was glad that at least we'd persuaded Alvaro to come along. Right now, he was down in the street below, waiting to be called up.

'He's the one who makes these heads,' Flossie went on, in that wide-eyed way of hers. 'I was just talking to my friend about how we were going to have to move out probably, and then I said Roderick Eaton's name and she said Alvaro – who's her dad, like I said – that he knew him, and it all came out. She says Eaton's violent, too – though he gets these other guys to beat people up. Apparently.'

Oh man, I thought. *Why didn't I say I'd do all the talking?*

Maro gazed at Flossie, clearly not convinced. 'OK, that's either completely made-up, or not the whole story,' she said. 'But I know you kids couldn't possibly have invented something as weird as this, so if it really is what Eaton is up to, we need to call the police.' She eyed each of us in turn, just to be sure.

Flossie turned bright-red.

It bothered me because it made it look as if the whole thing was a lie, instead of just the details about Alvaro. I decided we needed a small amount of confession.

'OK, we did do a bit of snooping,' I admitted. 'But

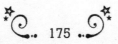

I promise we didn't do anything bad or dangerous…' (*Whoops!* I thought. *Little white lie there.*) 'And… we didn't say anything at the time…but you know when we went to that restaurant to celebrate Sam ditching the crutches? Well, we saw something…'

Maro's eyes widened. 'What? What did you see?'

'We saw a man being beaten up in the alleyway,' explained Sam.

Maro gasped.

'The thugs got away in the white van Eaton uses for deliveries,' Sam went on. 'I recognised it. But the victim insisted we mustn't tell anyone, so we didn't.'

'Yeah, but now we know this is about a lot more than just one man being duffed up,' I added. 'Look, this is just between us for now, OK? But I did a bit of homework…' I still had the internet piece about Mr Divine in my pocket. I took it out and showed it to her. 'That ghost at my school? This is him. See the part about the hit-and-run – the white van? They never did track down the driver, but we think it might be one of Eaton's guys.'

Maro frowned at the picture. 'But…I don't see–'

'Trust me. It all fits. Anyway, Alvaro's downstairs. Maybe you should talk to him.'

'He is?' said Maro. 'Well, get him up here!'

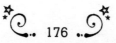

I went to fetch him.

Maro went over with Alvaro what we'd told her. He confirmed that we were telling the truth. Maro picked up the phone. 'Please stay here while I talk to the police.'

Alvaro looked nervous, in spite of what Sam had said. He put his hand out, as if to stop her. 'Maybe there's some other way? Like, an anonymous note, or something?'

Maro gave him one of those looks of hers that says, 'you've gotta be kidding'.

'Alvaro…kind of might be breaking the law himself,' I explained.

'Are you living here illegally?' Maro asked him.

'No,' said Alvaro.

'And you're no thug, I can see that,' said Maro. She had a knack for summing people up just by looking at them. She put the phone to her ear. 'Trust me, you have nothing to worry about.' She went ahead and made the call. This time Alvaro didn't try to stop her.

After she'd put the phone down, Maro announced, 'They'll be about half an hour. I'll make us some coffee.'

Just twenty minutes later, Maro answered the door to a woman police officer. She was kind of young-ish, with glossy dark hair scraped back off her face and

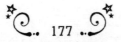

black-framed glasses. While Maro went about making another cup of coffee, Inspector Owen introduced herself to us. She smiled a lot, and insisted that we call her by her first name, Jacqueline. Even so, she was kind of scary in that police-y way. Alvaro looked uncomfortable as she took out her notepad and jotted down his name, address and telephone number.

'And how long have you known the Slade family?' she asked, not looking up from her pad.

'Erm…not very long,' said Alvaro.

Jacqueline blinked at him, smiling. 'Approximately?'

We all looked at each other. Oops. We hadn't worked out our story in enough detail.

'He's…a dad at my school?' said Flossie.

'Ah, right,' said Jacqueline. 'So…since nursery? Reception?'

We looked at each other again. Once again, Flossie's face was a total giveaway strawberry colour. Great – brilliant start. This wasn't going to work. We'd have to come clean.

I cleared my throat. 'Actually, only since today.'

'Ah-ha,' said Maro, folding her arms and nodding slowly.

'All right,' said Jacqueline. 'And…*how* did you meet?'

'We tracked him down,' I confessed, and between us

we explained about the beating we'd witnessed in the alleyway, and the link we'd made between the van, Pony and Baloney, and Eaton.

'Well, thank you for telling me about the beating incident,' said Jacqueline. 'But the link to your landlord is rather speculative, I'm afraid. I'd need a bit more to go on than this.'

'But...' I trailed off. I *so* didn't want to get into the whole thing with Rat-Man, or explaining my phantorama...

Instead I moved onto the stuff I'd overheard at Eaton Antiques. And as soon as I did, I realised I could also skip the meeting I'd arranged with Eaton on Maro's phone, and the trip to the restaurant. For now at least, I could let Jacqueline think I'd got all my info in the shop.

And then we came to the important bit: our visit to Alvaro's. No bypassing that one, unfortunately – although we'd agreed with Alvaro beforehand to say we'd only gone into his workroom after he'd let us all into the flat to look for the 'missing cat'. Which was kind of true, but also not true. All the same, we got a lecture about never going into strangers' homes.

The good thing was that none of it would get Alvaro into trouble, Jacqueline promised. 'At least, not for anything you've told me,' she added. 'You and your

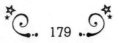

friends at the zoos will probably get off with a warning. It's not illegal to use the ape bodies for taxidermy. The only problem is that you didn't get a licence. Besides, if what you tell us about Mr Eaton is true, you'll be helping the police enormously by supplying information about him. We show our appreciation for things like that.'

Sam grinned at Alvaro. He'd been right.

'I am very relieved to hear that,' Alvaro said, looking pleased. But his smile quickly faded. 'Only…I am worried. Already Mr Eaton give me an order for another one of these heads, but I don't wan' to make it now. But if I refuse…I will be in big trouble.'

Jacqueline tapped her pen against her lips. 'Hmm… yes, I can well imagine. The difficulty is…to be frank with you, I'm afraid we still don't have a lot to go on here.'

My heart sank. 'We don't?'

Jacqueline adjusted her glasses. 'Unfortunately, you don't have proof that Mr Eaton is in fact selling these fake *tsantsas* for five-figure sums, pretending they're the real thing. He would simply deny what Sam says he overheard about the "deal" – his word against yours. Even the fact that we know Alvaro is supplying the heads doesn't prove that Eaton is guilty of fraud. We need hard evidence.'

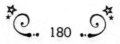

'But the guy's a crook!' cried Maro. 'There must be something you can do.'

Jacqueline bit her lip. 'Well…there might be. Have you ever heard of a "sting" operation?'

'I think so,' said Sam. 'You pretend you're a customer or something?'

'That's right,' said Jacqueline. She seemed surprised.

'Sam watches a *lot* of detective movies,' I explained.

'So here's what I'm thinking,' said Jacqueline. 'I would pose as a wealthy lady wanting to buy another of these *tsantsas* from Mr Eaton. Now, Alvaro, in order to do this, I must know as much as possible about the usual procedure. What do you know about Mr Eaton's dealings with his private clients?'

'I don't have much to do with that,' said Alvaro. 'But I know something about what happen. Like, you can't just call him up and say, "Hi, I want to buy a shrunken head." He is very careful. He have a special phone number. Only the people in the shop, they know. Even I don't know it. He told me all this himself, because he want me to know I won't get caught, because of…' Alvaro looked sheepish.

'Yes, yes, don't worry about that,' said Jacqueline, waving it off. 'Go on.'

'So maybe you can get the number from the shop, if

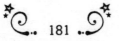

you are clever,' said Alvaro. 'Then the next thing is, you text him, and you got to use the code word. You don't use that word? No way he is dealing with you.'

Jacqueline leaned closer. 'And the word is…?'

Alvaro grinned. 'You are lucky. He ask me for a word – something in the language of the Jivaro, that nobody would use. So I give. The word is: "muisak".'

'Muzak?' said Jacqueline. 'Isn't that the sort of music they play in lifts and supermarkets?'

'No, "moo-iz-ack",' Alvaro explained. 'In the language of the Shuar, one of the Jivaroan tribes, this word mean "vengeful spirit". Muisak. That is the thing, the power in the enemy that the tribesmen took control of, when they shrunk their heads.'

'Like a genie in a bottle?' suggested Jacqueline.

'Kind of like that, yes,' said Alvaro. 'Oh, and you got to use the word in a sentence, in place of the word "music". "I'm interested in buying some music," or something – only you use "muisak" instead. Here–' He picked up a pen and scrawled the word on a scrap of paper. 'Important that you spell it right. This is why you text, not call. You see? Then he calls you back.' He handed Jacqueline the piece of paper.

Jacqueline gave a big smile. 'Excellent. Leave it with me.'

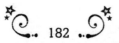

Don Thingummy

'I do so like a pot of Earl Grey mid-morning, don't you, Hilda?' said Hortense, sipping from the bone china cup.

'Yes, indeed. So refreshing!' agreed Hilda.

Groan. *Here we go again*, I thought. *Stuck with these two old biddies, right when there's serious investigating to be done.*

We were mooching around Eaton Antiques, pretending to browse – all of us this time, including Maro. We'd gone in a few minutes after Eaton had arrived, giving him time to disappear into the office at the back at the shop. By now he would be sitting there, ready and waiting for his new 'private client' – Jacqueline – to arrive.

Pony and Baloney were there too, moving some furniture up on the gallery. Outside, tucked around the side streets leading off Portobello Road, police officers

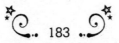

sat in their cars, waiting for the signal that it was time to move in.

I tried to avoid Hilda and Hortense, but it was a quiet morning at Eaton Antiques, and even from the other side of the shop I could still hear them wittering on about how much they missed taking tea in the garden, and why didn't these people put a few potted plants around the place to liven it up.

Tune them out, I told myself. Then Jacqueline appeared, and it suddenly became a whole lot easier.

'Oh wow, is that really her?' whispered Flossie.

I caught a whiff of expensive perfume as Jacqueline wafted past, not acknowledging us. 'Blimey! Yes, it is.'

She looked like she'd just stepped out of Selfridges or somewhere – a sort of female version of the Man In Black we'd seen in the restaurant. All bouffed-up hair, high-heeled boots, studded leather jacket and *serious* jewellery. The look said, 'I'm loaded with cash, and I'm a bit rock'n'roll, too'. The sort of person who likes to collect weird and revolting artifacts for their squillion-pound home. I saw Pony and Baloney watching her admiringly from up in the gallery.

We looked on as Jacqueline spoke to the grey-haired shop assistant, who then showed her to the back room.

Not long now.

Flossie sighed. 'I want to be in the police when I grow up. Not the boring everyday work, though, only sting operations and stuff.'

I clamped a hand over her mouth. 'Sshh! Don't mention the "S" word!'

'Sorry,' whispered Flossie. She sighed again and pretended to show interest in a cabinet full of china figurines.

I wandered next to Sam and Maro, who were gazing at the window display.

'Is there anything in particular you're interested in, madam?' asked the grey-haired man, ambling over.

'This mirror is unusual,' said Maro. 'How much is it?'

While Maro discussed mirrors with the shop assistant, Sam and I were in a good spot to keep an eye out for police officers in Portobello Road. That would be our first sign that Eaton had been successfully stung.

I pictured the scene right now in his office: him schmoozing away, spinning some impressive-sounding tale of his 'special source' for these 'extremely rare and highly prized antiques' or some such rubbish... Jacqueline asking to see a certificate of authentication, which he'd produce – a fake, of course. Then they'd agree on some massive five-figure price, and *boom!*

A discreet signal from Jacqueline, and the arrest would take place.

Any…minute…now…

Then, with Eaton convicted – hopefully Pony and Baloney as well – Rat-Man's business would be complete. He'd rest in peace at last…and leave *me* in peace. And we'd get to stay in our home!

This had to work. Nothing could go wrong, it mustn't…

My heart skipped a beat as I spotted flashes of uniform between the shoppers and the street stalls. At last – the police were here. We moved closer to the door, ready for the action.

Six of them came in. The poor old shop assistant didn't know what had hit him. 'Can I help you?' he asked nervously.

One of the policemen showed his ID. 'You have a Mr Roderick Eaton on the premises?'

The assistant's face turned grey, matching his hair. 'Er…well, yes, but he's in a meeting–'

'I know,' said the policeman. 'And this can't wait.'

The old guy scratched his ear. 'Right. This way, please.'

The first policeman and one other followed him to the back room. The other four stayed behind, and in a moment were clanking up the spiral staircase to the gallery – blocking Pony and Baloney as they tried to come down. The two thugs turned and dashed back along the gallery – which seemed kind of dumb, as there was no other way out from there.

At that moment the office door burst open. Out came a purple-faced Roderick Eaton, handcuffed and sandwiched between the two policemen, with Jacqueline behind him.

'This is absolutely outrageous!' he yelled. 'I am a respectable businessman and I demand to speak with my lawyer, right now!'

'When we get to the station, Mr Eaton,' said the officer.

Just then there was a shout from up in the gallery. Everyone gasped, staring in disbelief as Pony launched himself off the balcony and onto a crystal chandelier that was about the size of a small car. What he was thinking I don't know, but the next moment the whole thing came crashing down, along with half the ceiling – *smash!* – right on top of his boss and the police…

It was like a bomb had gone off.

Maro pulled us close to her. People were freaking out, and for a few moments I could barely see a thing as the place filled up with a massive cloud of dust.

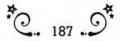

Gradually, some figures emerged, coughing, from under the glittering pile of plaster and crystal. One policeman, two policemen... Jacqueline struggled to free herself from under the chandelier, and Eaton...Eaton was just lying there, not moving. And Pony...where was Pony?

We rushed over to help Jacqueline. 'Oh my god, where'd he go?' I said. 'Where's Pony?'

One of the policemen pushed the chandelier off Jacqueline and quick as a flash, she wriggled free. 'One of the porters has got away,' she called into her walkie-talkie as she gazed around wildly. 'Repeat, one of the...correction, *both* of the porters have got away, over...'

Oh no – Baloney too? *How the hell?*

'Surround the property, over!' yelled Jacqueline.

Suddenly I felt an icy draught, and a twisted, echoing sound vibrated right through me. I covered my ears, then saw a rat scuttle across my feet. My eye followed it until I saw Rat-Man. He was howling at me, and now I knew why – beside him was Eaton, not only conscious but already up on his knees, in spite of having his hands cuffed behind his back. He hoisted himself to his feet and hurtled for the door. A policeman lurched over and tried to block his way, but Eaton rammed through head-first like a human bullet. We ran after him.

Outside, a crowd of idiot gawpers were lapping up the drama, all crowded round the shop, and like sheep, they actually started to *make way* for Eaton as he thundered out. *Duh!*

'Don't let him get away!' I yelled, but everyone just looked confused, like they were wondering whose side they were meant to be on.

We had to do something NOW, to BLOCK HIS WAY... Next thing I knew, Sam went round and threw himself at the huge wooden Beefeater but it barely moved until...yes! Rat-Man was there too, giving it every gram of his not-very-great strength, and with another shove from Sam it toppled over, *cre-e-e-eak, thunk!* Right in Eaton's way. That blocked him just long enough to give Flossie the chance to grab hold of the handcuff chain and give it a good yank.

'Aargh!' yelled Eaton, falling backwards.

This time, he was helpless. He was on his back, legs flailing like some joke old-geezer version of a break-dancer.

The policemen caught up; at the same time, more squad cars arrived at the scene, sirens blaring as they gently nudged their way through the crowds. Eaton was surrounded.

I dashed back inside, where it was still chaos.

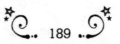

'The porters,' Jacqueline yelled again into her walkie-talkie. 'Do we have the porters, over!'

'*No sign of them out here,*' came the staticky response. '*We've got the van covered, over.*'

Jacqueline searched the room. 'Damn! Where did they get to?'

I glanced around for Rat-Man, but he'd disappeared. No doubt the effort of helping topple the Beefeater had used up all his energy. There'd be no more from him now.

The police were questioning the few stunned shoppers who were still there, but they didn't know where Pony and Baloney had gone either. 'I just ducked for cover when that chandelier came down,' said one.

'I don't know if–' another began, but his voice was drowned out by the sound of *clapping*, of all things, behind me.

I turned and saw Hilda and Hortense, looking utterly thrilled. 'Bravo, bravo!' they cried. 'At *last*, a bit of drama!'

'Shut *up*!' I snapped, but all it got me were strange looks, and Hilda and Hortense didn't hear, as usual. Oh, tune them out, *tune them out*…

'One does so miss the theatre,' said Hilda. She pronounced it 'the-*etter*'.

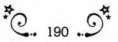

'Marvellous,' agreed Hortense. 'Frightful amount of damage!' she added gleefully.

I concentrated hard on what the witnesses were saying, and finally the ghosts' voices started to fade. Then – hang on – weren't Hilda and Hortense witnesses too? What was more, they hadn't had to duck for cover…

I hastily tuned back in. '…like the end of Don Thingummy, when he descends into hell!' Hilda was saying.

Argh! What had I missed?

'You mean Don Giovanni,' said Hortense.

'Yes, that's it!' said Hilda. 'I remember a magnificent performance by…'

Never mind that! I thought, as they wittered on. All I could do was stare hard and *will* them to say something relevant.

'I say, do you think those chaps'll come back up for an encore?' said Hortense, nudging her friend. The two of them giggled hysterically.

Aha! 'Back up'? From where? The shop had no basement level, so there were no stairs…was there a trapdoor somewhere nearby? I searched the rug-strewn floor desperately. It didn't seem likely. Surely a rug would have slipped off if a trapdoor underneath it had

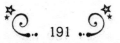

been opened? Not knowing what else to do, I kneeled down and felt under the fringes of the rugs – yes! Here was an edge…and a handle, set into the wood. The rug over the trapdoor was stapled down.

'Hey!' I called out. 'I think I've found something!'

Ice Spirit

In another couple of minutes, it was all over.

Eaton was caught. Pony and Baloney were caught.

Mission accomplished.

I was right. Amazingly, the two guys had somehow got themselves down into the cellar. We were told later that right after Pony jumped, Baloney had flipped over the banisters and jumped down, colliding with a set of dining chairs. Both were injured but they were tough guys and guilty as hell...the dust cloud hid them from view as they made a beeline for the trapdoor. Hearing the police come down after them, they'd scrambled to the back, where more steps led up directly into the courtyard. But of course, more police were waiting for them there – Pony and Baloney had no escape.

The story was all over the news the next day. Eaton was

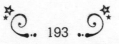

being done for serious fraud. Result!

That evening, we were all sitting and watching the six o'clock news, ready for the latest update. There was a clip of Eaton being escorted by the police – typically, grinning at the camera like a stupid Beefeater, as if he was being awarded a prize or something. Apparently he was going to deny everything in court and plead not guilty.

'But he doesn't have a foot to stand on,' Maro said.

'Leg,' I said. 'He doesn't have a *leg* to stand on.'

'Right,' she said. 'He doesn't have that either.'

'*Two employees of Mr Eaton's have been charged for assaulting police officers,*' said the TV announcer. '*They are also being questioned about their involvement in the fraudulent dealings, and a possible further assault...*'

'And a killing!' I yelled at the telly. 'What about the killing?'

'But, Kitty, you never told Jacqueline about the hit-and-run, remember?' said Sam.

'But…but they've *got* Pony and Baloney! All they have to do is–'

'What? Question them about Rat-Man? They can't do that if they don't know about him.'

Urgh. How was I going to explain all of that, without having to tell the world about my phantorama?

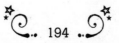

Just then, the door buzzer went. 'Oh, who is that?' said Maro, irritated. She got up and answered the intercom. 'Hello? Who? Oh. Well…why are you here? No, not really… Oh, all right.' She buzzed the visitor into the building.

'Who is it?' asked Flossie.

'Mr Wesley.'

I stood up and zapped off the TV. 'Mr *Wesley*? What, as in Mr Wesley, my old science teacher?'

Maro shrugged. 'I tried to get rid of him, but–'

The doorbell rang. I disappeared into my bedroom – here was someone I did *not* want to see. Sam and Floss joined me, and we huddled by my bedroom door and listened.

'I'm sorry if it's a bad time, Mrs Slade,' said Mr Wesley. 'I won't keep you long. But I've tried several times to call, and haven't been able to get hold of you. And…well, something's happened at the school that I think you should be aware of.'

Uh-oh, I thought. Floss, Sam and I looked at each other nervously. Had our sneaking into the school been reported?

'Can I get you anything, Mr Wesley?' Maro didn't sound bothered at all. 'Some tea? Coffee?'

'No, no, that's all right, Mrs Slade.'

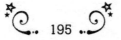

'Please, have a seat.'

'Thank you.' Mr Wesley cleared his throat. 'Ahem, well, you see…this is rather hard to believe, I know, but…' He trailed off for a moment, then started again. 'The fact is, Mrs Slade, that it appears that your granddaughter might have seen some sort of…uh, *apparition*, in class that day after all.'

I stared at Flossie and Sam. This was not what I'd expected at all. Interesting…

'Ah!' said Maro. 'Well of course, Mr Wesley, I never doubted that for a moment.'

I moved out of my hiding place and back into the living room. Mr Wesley looked at me sheepishly, and fiddled with his tie. 'Oh, hello, Kitty. I was just explaining to your grandmother that—'

'Yes, I know,' I said, sitting down.

'Well now, I hope you can appreciate that, from our perspective, this was absolutely the least likely explanation for your behaviour in class that day.'

'What happened, then?' I asked. It was fun to watch him squirm. 'Did someone else see him?'

'Not exactly,' said Mr Wesley, staring at the carpet near my feet. 'But some strange things have been happening. First of all, there was some sort of intrusion. I have to be honest, I did suggest to the police that you

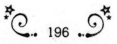

might be the culprit, Kitty.'

I didn't avert my eyes. *Remember the body language*, I told myself. Don't give yourself away. One look at Flossie or Sam, and Mr Wesley might be onto us.

'Was anything stolen?' asked Maro.

'No,' said Mr Wesley. 'There was a small amount of damage, but that's it – even though they got into a cupboard that contained some pretty valuable items. But it seems the intruders were nearly caught by the caretaker, so they beat a hasty retreat. Unfortunately, nothing has been caught on camera.'

'What sort of items?' asked Maro.

'Before I go into that,' said Mr Wesley, 'let me tell you about the subsequent strange events. You see, ever since the intrusion, there has been a strange… atmosphere in that lab. It's icy cold, even with the heating on, but it's not just that. There's more to it. It's…I can't really describe it…'

'*To pnevma payon*,' said Maro.

Mr Wesley frowned. 'I'm sorry…?'

'What we Greeks would call the "ice spirit". Were the electrics affected?'

'Yes!' said Mr Wesley. 'The lights wouldn't stop buzzing and flickering. We got an electrician in, but he couldn't find out what was causing it. But most of all there

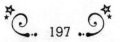

was this sense of dread…everyone who went in there experienced it. Oh, it seems so clichéd, and I never would have believed it if I hadn't witnessed it for myself. So we had to close up the lab. We couldn't use it for lessons.'

Obviously Rat-Man, I thought. Only once the lab was closed up – and I was no longer around – he'd had to track me down at home, hadn't he?

'What were the things in the cupboard?' asked Maro.

'Are you familiar with the term "rogue taxidermy"?' asked Mr Wesley.

'Well, I know about taxidermy, of course,' said Maro. 'But the "rogue" part, no.'

The rest of us just hung in there, adopting what we hoped were curious expressions.

'All it means is that someone has taken parts of different animals – a rat and a fish, for example,' Mr Wesley went on. 'And put them together, to form sort of mythic beasts. There were several such creatures in display cases, hidden away in the cupboard. You see, when I first started working there, I was told not to use that cupboard as it was being used for long-term storage. I didn't even have a key.' He shrugged. 'I thought nothing of it. Anyway, the haunting – I can think of no other way to describe it – well, it turns out that this has happened before.'

Wow. Unexpected statement number two.

'Really?' I said.

Mr Wesley nodded. 'You see, it seems the stuffed creatures were made by my predecessor, Mr Divine. Following Divine's accidental death, the head teacher discovered them in the cupboard. But when he tried to move them, the same thing happened. There was the cold, the sense of dread…the problem with the lights. And when he put them back, locked them away, everything went back to normal. The difference this time is that even after I locked them away again, the haunting, uh…hasn't stopped.'

He looked at me, as if *I* had the answer. Ha! Did he actually think I'd be able to *exorcise* the ghost?

'It's a worry, I don't mind telling you,' he went on. 'There's a schools inspector visiting next week. If anything…untoward happens, I shudder to think…'

Hmm…it was possible that Rat-Man had calmed down a bit, now that Eaton and his cronies were caught. He hadn't appeared to me last night, at least. But the school wouldn't know that, if no one had been back into the lab to check. Of course, he might start haunting all over again if Pony and Baloney got away without being charged for the hit-and-run… Oh wow – I *so* had to fix that.

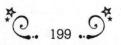

199

Mr Wesley stood up. 'Anyway, the point is, I just wanted to apologise for any misunderstanding about what happened in class. I'm not sure how it was that you saw something that nobody else did, Kitty – but then I don't understand the paranormal, anyway. We scientists can explain so much, but…not this. And I've come to let you know that your suspension has been revoked.'

I blinked at him. 'I'm sorry…?'

Mr Wesley beamed at me. 'We'd like to welcome you back, Kitty.'

I stared at him. Did I want to go back? In a way it would be good to see everyone again, but…life had changed so much. 'Um…'

Maro stood up. 'Thank you, Mr Wesley, but Kitty's being home-schooled now.'

The smile dropped from his face. 'I beg your pardon?'

'Yes, I am,' I said, my mind turning over. 'But I tell you what – I will see if I can get rid of the ghost for you.'

Mr Wesley looked surprised. 'Get *rid* of it? You can do that?'

I studied my fingernails, all nonchalant. 'I might be able to – in a day or so. I'm kind of busy.'

'Any time,' said Wesley. 'You just let us know, OK? And, uh…mum's the word, understood?' he added,

putting his finger to his lips. 'The…inspection, and everything…'

'I won't tell a *soul*,' I said.

Maro saw him out.

The minute he was gone, I jumped up and dived for the phone. 'Jacqueline? We've just been given some important new information that you need to know about.'

A couple of days later, we went along to the school, the whole family. It felt weird going there as a visitor – really weird.

But now I was ready for it.

After I'd told Jacqueline about Rat-Man and his monsters, the investigation had taken an interesting new turn. And I didn't even have to say a *word* about my phantorama. I just told her what Wesley had said about the break-in at the school, and what was found in the cupboard. Also the story about the hit-and-run – which they had on file, of course, but would never in a million years have linked to Eaton before now. It was thanks to the grey-haired dude from the shop that they had the final connection. He'd known about Eaton's deals, but had no idea he was conning people. He was shocked. And he had contact details of Eaton's suppliers

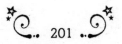

going back a number of years, including those of one Mr Divine...

The final connection was made – the net was closing in on Eaton and his henchmen.

And here we were, at Gateshill School, ready for a bit of fun.

As we headed over to the science wing, I turned to Mr Wesley. 'Can I have the key, please? I have to do this on my own.'

'Well, I'm not sure that's exactly–'

'I can't do it with anyone else there,' I told him, deadly serious. 'It's distracting for the spirits, you know.' I made sure not to catch Sam and Floss's eye, or I'd have cracked up.

Wesley hesitated. 'All right,' he said at last. 'But no...'

I stared at him. *No what?*

He averted his eyes. 'Good, good. Well...we'll just wait in the staff room. Is there, um, anything you need?'

Crucifix? I thought. *Magic wand?* 'No, thanks,' I said brightly.

'All right, well...good luck.' He still looked a bit worried. You could tell that deep down he didn't trust me.

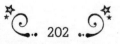

What do you think I'm gonna do? I thought. *Set the place on fire?* But I just thanked him, and went on my way.

Arriving at the lab door, I hesitated. What I would do if the lab was still haunted, I didn't know…it had better not be. But even though I felt sure Rat-Man would be satisfied now, there was still that niggling doubt. I mean, it wasn't as if he'd thanked me or anything. Which, come to think of it, was a bit rude of him.

Oh well, I thought. *Here goes.* I unlocked the door and went in.

Everything seemed…normal. It was chilly, yes – but then the heating was turned off. And no 'sense of dread' that I could detect. I turned on the lights. They flickered at first, the way fluorescents do – but once they were fully on, no flickering. I was all alone – just me, the lab, and the soft hum of the lights.

Suddenly, there was a loud buzzing-and-bleeping noise, which made me jump out of my skin. Then I realised it was coming from my pocket. It was my phone. Someone was texting me.

Sam.

Maro just heard from jac. Pony and baloney confessed to manslaughter of rat-man. Also the beating. Yay!

Brilliant.

'OK, Rat-Man,' I yelled. 'I hope you're satisfied at last. Check it out!' I held the phone up. Such a pointless thing to do, but hey, you do weird things in weird situations.

Time to go. Soon this whole part of the story would be reported in the news, and no one would ever know whether Kitty Slade had exorcised the spirit of the science lab, or if he'd gone of his own accord once his killers had been brought to justice. For now, I could have my moment of glory. I called Maro on her phone, and told her they could come down now.

I didn't expect them *all* to come. There was not only Wesley, but the head teacher, and Grindley, and a bunch of others.

'Marvellous!' proclaimed the head teacher, striding around the room. 'At last! We can use the lab again. Kitty, I have no idea what you did here, but whatever it is, I'm grateful...really grateful! Now, Mrs Slade, when will Kitty be joining us again?'

'I've already told Mr Wesley that she won't be, sir,' said Maro.

'Oh?'

'No. You see, we're moving.'

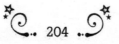

I gawped at her. 'We are? But I thought…' Surely we didn't have to move now that Eaton wouldn't be taking over the flat? That was the whole point of…like, everything!

Maro smiled. 'Oh, it's something we need to discuss, of course. But the new home I had in mind would be of the four-wheeled variety – a camper van. So, er…literally moving!'

There was an ear-splitting squeal, which I soon realised had come from Flossie.

'Does that mean I get to quit school as well?' Flossie asked.

'Yes!' said Maro. Then, noticing the teachers' disapproving looks, she added, 'I'm well-versed in home-schooling, you know.'

'Where will we go?' I asked.

'All over the country,' said Maro. 'From Land's End to John O'Groats. And Europe, too. We can go where we like, and our home comes with us.'

Unexpected statement number three!

The Hippo

Just two weeks later we were out on the street, waiting eagerly for the delivery of our new home.

Yep – it was that simple. Of course, Maro did consult us properly and she apologised for announcing her idea out of the blue.

'No, it was brilliant,' I said. 'I wouldn't have missed the look on old Wesley's face for the world!'

Sam and Flossie agreed, and Maro explained how the idea had come about. 'I was working out where we could afford to move to,' she said. 'I'm not rich, God knows…but I've lived a long time and I had a bit of money saved up. But…not that much. That's when I hit on the idea of a camper van – the only sort of home I could afford to buy outright. Of course, now that Eaton's going to prison, we're free to stay…but I've realised that I don't really want to. I've been bitten by

the travel bug! What do you all think?'

It was a no-brainer.

Maro had got out a bunch of road atlases, and showed us all the places she thought we'd visit. 'I don't see enough of *to ikogenia*, the family,' she said. And it was true. Aside from the one aunt in London we saw all the time, there were others that we hardly ever saw. There was the aunt in Cornwall, the uncle in Scotland – and their families, of course. Then there were all the ones in Greece. This way we could visit them for as long as we wanted, without using up space in their homes. And Maro had loads of friends all over the place as well. She hardly ever saw them, either.

'What is the point of having friends if you never spend time with them?' she said.

We'd go where we wanted, when we wanted. I couldn't wait! I didn't even care that we had to get rid of loads of stuff – like a space shuttle breaking away from its rocket, we'd be this compact little capsule with just enough stuff to get by. Even Sam came round to the idea, once he was allowed to bring at least part of his beloved library and DVD collection.

As for Flossie, she was delighted not to be the only one still going to school. 'Are you sure though, *pethaki-mou*?' Maro had asked. 'You like school.'

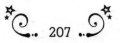

'Just 'cause I like *that* school, doesn't mean I prefer it to no school at all,' said Flossie. And she'd never liked ballet much.

So it was settled; there really was nothing holding us back.

And here we were, on a breezy March morning, waiting for the camper van.

'Be careful now, don't scratch it!' I heard a familiar voice cry out, and I turned to see Hilda, the Eaton Antiques ghost, leaving the shop. She was trotting alongside the new deliveryman, who was wheeling away her beloved dresser. Behind them, Hortense, short and squat in her bustled skirt, was also keeping track of the progress of her precious writing desk.

I waved to them. 'Bye, guys! Have fun!'

But they didn't answer, of course. Never mind, I was glad they were going to find proper homes at last.

'Who are you talking to?' asked Flossie.

'Just some ghosts.'

'Oh.' Flossie rolled her eyes.

'Eaton Antiques is history!' said Sam, as the deliveryman passed by. After Eaton's dramatic departure, the 'Closing-down Sale' signs had soon gone up and all of a sudden, they were doing a roaring trade. The shop was emptying out.

'Yes, and all the money will go straight into the pockets of Eaton's defence lawyers, no doubt,' said Maro. Then she glanced up. 'Oh, look! Here it comes!'

A big fat lumbering white whale of a thing was trundling up the road. Our new home. We went completely hyper, bouncing around and whooping. Well, it was exciting!

We went right on bouncing inside the thing – as soon as it had, like, stopped and everything. The van had that new smell even though it was second-hand. Sort of plasticky, but in a good way. Maro went to wrap up the business side of things with the seller person.

'Oh, brilliant,' I said. 'It's like a Tardis!'

'Er, not really,' said Sam.

'OK, OK, I know, not *literally*…but it's cool, isn't it? Look at the little kitchen…the shower cubicle. It's all so…dinky! What's that, Floss?'

Flossie was messing around with the sliding door to the loo. 'Now you see me, now you don't…now you see me–'

'Hey, look, Floss, this is where you and I sleep!' I said, remembering the pictures Maro had shown us and folding back the dining table.

Sam was looking at his bed. 'It's a bit…small.'

'But cool!'

'Hey, Sam, we're gonna be outside most of the time anyway,' said Flossie.

Sam grinned. 'I know. Yeah, it is great. Just…no bugging me at night, OK?'

'Yeah, whatever.'

Maro bounced inside, just as excited as the rest of us. 'Well, kids, what do you think?'

'Amazing!'

'Awesome!'

'Small…but beautiful.'

'Hey, I thought of a name for it,' said Maro. 'The Hippo.'

Sam scrunched up his face. 'The Hippo?'

'As in *Doureos hippos,* which is Greek for Trojan horse,' explained Maro, getting all carried away. 'Only we'll be like a *friendly* version of the Trojans, of course. We'll roll into town under cover of night, then *leap out* and surprise everyone the next morning!'

'We will?'

'Well, sort of,' said Maro. 'A bit. Only we'll phone ahead. Maybe. Anyway, it has to have a name and I like the Hippo.'

'I thought "hippo" meant hippo, not horse,' said Flossie.

'Ah, no: "hippopotamus" comes from the Greek for

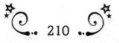

"water horse",' said Maro. 'The hippo part means horse. There you go – your language lesson for the day. Let nobody say you won't be getting an education. OK, help me load up, kids.'

'What's in here?' asked Flossie, peering into a shopping bag Maro had just put down.

'I almost forgot,' said Maro. 'Some going-away presents for you!'

Maro took out the packages and handed them to us.

There were DVDs, including the box set of Hitchcock movies Sam had wanted. There were clothes, including a brand-new pair of dancing shoes for Flossie. 'So you can learn other dances a bit more fun than ballet,' said Maro. And there was one other thing as well...

GHOST BLOG
TUESDAY 29 MARCH

Composed on the brand-new laptop!

Well, I didn't think I'd be blogging again so soon. Was thinking, that's it – no more Rat-Man. Which I was WELL RELIEVED about, let me tell you.

BUT…just now, I saw him. We're leaving town in a

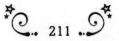

couple of hours, off to start our new life. We've been getting some food in, and I was heading over to the market to buy some bananas when I thought I saw him – tall, thin, grey-faced as ever, standing stock still in the crowd, staring at me. I blinked, and he was gone. So I carried on…then there he was again! Same as before, just standing there. Then gone again.

So next thing is, I'm queuing at the fruit stall, and there's bits of rubbish on the ground – you know, like there always is in markets. And I'm idly watching the scraps of paper and stuff scudding about, when all of a sudden they swirl around and form themselves into the words 'thank you'!

Can you believe it?

So I'm staring at this thing, and then there he is again, standing beside the stall, facing me. The sky's still murky grey, but suddenly it's like he's been hit by a beam of sunlight from nowhere, making him glow, shimmer…then dissolve into nothing. And the words on the ground are lifted up and shuffled back into no meaning.

And I know he's gone for good. That was it – Rat-Man's farewell. Hey, I got thanked by a ghost! How cool is that? His unfinished business got finished, and I was the one who made that possible.

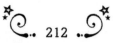

Number three stupid thing people say about ghosts: They don't thank you for sorting out their problems.

OK, people DON'T say that. But they also don't say that they DO, which amounts to the same thing.

Oh damn. Just realised, I forgot to buy the bananas.

Glossary of Maro-isms

To vrathi [to **vra**-thi]......dinner

Piyainete! [pee-**yen**-et-ay]......go away!

Vlakas! [**vlak**-ass]......idiot!

Pethaki-mou [pe-**tha**-ki moo]......my little child

Agapi-mou [a-**gah**-pee moo]......my love

Kitaki-mou [Kit-**ak**-I moo]......my little Kitty

Flosaki-mou [Flos-**ak**-I moo]......my little Flossie

O vromoskilos! [o vro-**mos**-kee-los]......the dirty dog!

Pos tolmas! [poss tol-**mas**]......how dare he!

To pnevma payon [to **pnev**-ma pa-**yon**]......ice spirit

To ikogenia [to ee-ko-**gen**-ee-ah]......family

Acknowledgements

My thanks once again to my husband Pano – for putting up with me when my head was elsewhere, rendering me incapable of intelligible conversation. Thanks to him also, along with Andros Epaminondas and Maria Psemada, for help with the Greek. Thanks as ever to my cousin Mat for help with police-related stuff. Thanks to my friends Lee Weatherly, Candy Gourlay, Keren David and Jo Kenrick; Kitty was messing with my head for a while, but you girls helped me knock her into shape! Thanks also to my fellow Sassies who have been so wonderfully supportive; you know who you are. x

Read on for an exclusive extract of *Fire and Roses*!

I lay there for a bit, just staring into the darkness above me, the way you do when you're listening out for something in the night. Why do we do that? As if staring will somehow make you hear better…

Then there was another little tinkle-smash sound… then another.

Everyone else just slept on.

I got up and went to the window. There was nothing to see out there, but when the sound came again – was it glass being smashed? – I could get a better sense of where it was coming from. And I was pretty sure it was coming from Dinky's house. Silently, I slipped into my sneakers and pulled on my hoody. Then, taking the keys from the hook by the door, I stepped outside, shutting the Hippo door as quietly as I could behind me. I crept right up to the house, close to the living room window at the front. But the curtains were drawn, so there was nothing to see…then came the sound again – louder this time. Definitely sounded like smashing glass. I snuck around the side of the house, pulling my hoody tightly around me; it was chilly.

The kitchen had these French windows, so I could get a good view inside. Of course it was dark, but between the cold blue light of the moon, and the warm orangey light coming from the hallway, I could pretty much make stuff out. Enough to see the mess on the floor: glinting shards of glass.

I thought about the dog, Hetty – perhaps she'd knocked something over by accident? But I couldn't see her anywhere in the kitchen…and anyway, there had been a whole series of these little smashes. Which you'd think would kind of indicate they were deliberate.

I was staring at the shattered glass on the floor, when out of the corner of my eye something whooshed by, then *smash!* On the floor, another glass. I turned to where it had whooshed from, and then came another, flying off the shelf…then another.

And nobody was there; the glasses were flying off the shelf all by themselves. And the shelf was perfectly level.

What the hell was going on? And if there was a ghost, how come I couldn't see it?

I wondered about Hetty again. How come she wasn't going nuts, barking her head off? For that matter, what about everyone else? Hadn't the noise woken any of them up?

I heard Hetty whining – I could see the shape of her now, a dark shadow, moving in the hallway. Poor thing – she was terrified. Too scared to bark.

Another glass: *smash*. And another one.

Then I caught a glimpse of white bathrobe moving down the stairs, and I hid myself. The kitchen light went on, and I heard Dinky's voice: 'Oh, Hetty, there, there!'

A muffled voice came from somewhere else in the house – Emily?

'It's nothing, darling: just a shelf that's come down. Go back to bed, sweetie,' Dinky said.

A shelf that's come down? That wasn't what happened. Dinky was lying. Why?

Don't miss the stunning new series from Holly Webb,
bestselling author of *Rose*

Magic will always find a way...

In a world where magic is
outlawed, Lily runs wild and
neglected. Once rich and
powerful magicians, now
Lily's family hide away in
their crumbling house, while
her older sister, Georgie, is
trained secretly in magic.

But when Lily discovers her
parents' dark plan to use
Georgie in a terrible plot to
restore the country to its
magical glory, she knows
she must rescue her sister –
and flee...

978 1 40831 349 7 £5.99 PB Oct 2011

ORCHARD BOOKS
www.orchardbooks.co.uk